WHEN A

# CAROL CITY

# THUG

LOVES YOU

A STANDALONE BY:

**TASHA MARIE**

# SYNOPSIS

Although Peyton wasn't raised in the hood, she quickly adapted when she met the notorious Faheem, Carol City's finest. Over the years, being tied to the plug with successful businesses all over Miami has bossed up her life. However, all the finer things and an expensive ring can't hide the fact that's she's missing a genuine love and affection. Peyton plays the fool and chance after chance, Faheem slides back in her good graces. After a near tragic incident involves the kindness of a southern gangsta, she soon realizes she needs to walk away for good.

It's been eight long years and Syncere's ready to pump the streets with his full attention after giving the Florida prison system so much time of his life. Almost overnight, he upgrades from a DOC jumpsuit to designer clothes once he's introduced to the head honcho of the streets. After telling himself it's, "money over everything", a run in with a feisty chick quickly changes that plan. He's instantly drawn to Peyton and while their chemistry is undeniable from the start, Syncere struggles with getting her to leave her current situation once and for all.

They say the realest love comes around when you need it the most but, how easy is letting go when you're affiliated with such a powerful man? Love can be complex and dangerous, especially When A Carol City Thug Loves You. In the end, will love prevail? Read along to find out and experience the drama, pain, betrayal and bloodshed as the streets turn up.

# CHAPTER ONE

# PEYTON

"Hello?"

"Yeah, this Peyton?"

"Who wants to know?"

"Girl, please. I know who you are, but you don't know me. Listen here, I been fuckin' with Faheem for a lil' minute now and guess what, sis, I'm pregnant! So, tell that fine ass fiancé of yours he better pay up for this abortion or we all gon' be one blended ass family in about six months, ya heard! He better stop ignoring my calls! Okay sis?" *CLICK!*

"Damn, girl. Who the fuck was that?"

I placed my phone in my purse and took a few deep breaths before I snapped. My hands were shaking and my heart was pounding as sweat formed on my top lip. This shit was getting real old and downright embarrassing! Heem was steady embarrassing me and I was legit sick to my stomach about it. This was the third call today from a blocked number and of course while I was out browsing through wedding dresses, I just so happened to answer the fucking call. Silly me. I stood in the dressing room in a five hundred-thousand-dollar wedding dress with my eyes closed, fists balled, counting down from ten.

"Hello! Earth to Peyton. You alright?"

Once I gathered my composure, I opened my eyes to see my best friend Milah and my older sister, Paris staring me down with worry. I sighed. "I'm alright, y'all. Let's just go. Unzip me please. Just unzip me." I wanted to get the fuck away from everybody, curl up in a ball and die.

"Go?" Paris questioned with an eyebrow raised. "We just got here. You only tried on this one dress, baby sister."

"Right." Milah added on. "What's up with you? Who called you?" She placed her hands on her hips.

"I just wanna go home! Damn!" I spazzed on them and turned my back as the tears fell. Quietly, I said, "Just unzip me please."

I didn't want to mention the phone call. I was tired of looking stupid and in that moment, I felt like the dumbest bitch alive. I was pretty as shit; brown skin with a pixie cut I kept low and sometimes with different colors, real perky titties and my ass to thigh ratio was on point. I was southern thick. People say I resembled the actress Malinda Williams from the movie The Wood. There wasn't shit fake about me including my inner being. I was about as real of a woman as they came. I was Faheem's peace and constantly he made me feel like just a piece.

See, I knew he wasn't perfect and that was something I came to realize from jump. I mean, with good looks, hella street cred and crazy bank, how could any woman expect him to be faithful? He was the king of these Miami streets. There wasn't a single ounce of any drug moving through Carol City without him knowing about it or signing off on it. When I met him eight years ago, I was drawn to his bad boy lifestyle being that I lived the complete opposite. I came from money but when I saw him, I saw hella dollar signs, a dangerous vibe and a way out of my prima donna lifestyle. I didn't care if he had other women as long as I was taken care of financially and sexually. Faheem did just that and then some.

He cuffed me and slapped a ring on it after just two years of seeing each other off and on. He told me I was his number one and that I always would be. Promising to cut off his hoes so we could be exclusive out here, I believed him. He bought us the biggest mansion in the hood to give all the niggas something to talk about then got us matching Rovers and Rollies to stunt with. It didn't take long for word to spread that Faheem was officially off the market. Aside from some family conflicts, life was great. Envy came from all over Miami-Dade County and I embraced it. We took trips overseas every other month and threw the biggest parties that brought the whole city out. He was that nigga and I was his bitch and soon to be wife. You couldn't tell me shit.

That is until one day I pulled my car into the garage and saw this chick sitting on my front steps with a car seat on her lap. I approached her to see if she was lost, and she told me I clearly was the lost one. Her name was Whitney and the baby, Faheem Shamir Jr, was four months old at the time. As much as I wanted to drag this hoe, I couldn't. The baby was my fiancé's twin and there was no denying that. I could never explain the hurt and disappointment I felt that day. Unless you've been in my shoes, you could never understand the heartache. It was all my fault though. I opened that door from the beginning for Faheem to do him and when I tried to close it, he obviously left it cracked a little bit.

Over the years, I'd fought bitches, stabbed one and beat a couple of cases. Then, on top of that, this muthafucka had two kids on me. I was looking like stepmother of the decade because I still hadn't gotten pregnant by him; not that I was trying to for validation or anything. Hell, I knew a baby didn't keep a nigga nor did a ring. I just couldn't walk away though. I refused to let these bitches have him after the blood, sweat and tears I'd put in. A man will only do what you allow him to do and for years I'd been allowing Faheem to break my spirit and tear me down emotionally. I loved him and despite all the bullshit, I knew he loved me just as deeply. We had a rare type of love. I kept telling myself one day he would see the good woman I was and really leave these hoes alone. In the passenger seat of Milah's car, I twirled my fat ass engagement ring and sadly hoped he'd get it together one day.

***

I slid my key in the front door and was automatically met with heavy weed smoke and loud trap music. After the afternoon I'd just had, I definitely wasn't in the mood for this type of atmosphere. I tossed my keys on the glass table by the door and slid my Giuseppe's off.

"What's good, baby?" Faheem greeted me with a blunt hanging from his lips.

"'Sup sis?"

"What it do, P?"

Faheem's slow ass brother, Saige and their homeboy Teddy gave me a head nod as their fingers worked the PS4 joysticks. All eyes were glued to the 70-inch plasma that hung on the wall. A bottle of D'Ussé and red cups were on the marble coffee table before them as they turned up and played that damn NBA 2K video game. I hated the shit and wanted to break every last game he had, including the fucking system. Ever since I was younger, I couldn't stand how dudes would become so engrossed in a video game and block the rest of the world out. Somehow though, Faheem managed to run the city, play video games, please me and hump around. My thoughts circled back to the phone call earlier and a lump formed in my throat.

"Hey y'all," I greeted them all back dryly and rolled my eyes at Faheem's ass. I kept it moving past the couch and into the kitchen to pour me up a glass of something strong. I needed it. I chose Patron mixed with lemonade and gulped the entire glass down like it was nothing. Lately I'd been drinking more and more, but I didn't care. It numbed the pain to say the least.

"Baby, you didn't hear me calling you?" Faheem snuck up on me from behind and hugged my waist. He started sucking on my neck, and I could feel his dick getting hard. I could also smell the liquor coming from his pores and my stomach automatically turned. One thing about him, when he drank, he got super drunk on every occasion.

I pushed him away with my backside and turned my nose up. "Heem, stop. I'm not in the mood." I poured myself a shot of Patron and threw it back before turning around to face him. His eyes were blood shot. I shook my head in disgust.

He licked his lips and rubbed his chin. "And why is that? Didn't you go out dress shopping today? It went bad or something?" Even though I was pissed, I looked at him from eye to toe think-

11

ing, *why he gotta be so damn fine?* Faheem was half Trinidadian and half Black with smooth brown skin, deep dimples and long wavy hair, which he usually rocked in two braids. He was fine as fuck and his full beard was always on point. He was slim with a nice build but don't sleep, the slimmer the nigga, the bigger his dick. It wasn't just a myth. Hence, why he was slanging the shit all up and through Miami!

I chuckled. "Or something…" I shook my head and then eyeballed him up and down once more. "You still don't know how to keep your dick in your pants huh, Faheem?"

"What?" His eyebrows shot up like he was appalled by my accusation.

"Nigga, don't what me!" I shouted. "I got a call today from another bitch who claims she's pregnant with Faheem's baby." I clapped my hands and laughed a little bit. "Congrats, my nigga. Congrats again." The look on his face told me he knew exactly what bitch I was talking about. The guilt could be smelled coming from his pores as well.

He reached for me. "P…"

I slapped his hands away as the tears fell from my eyes. "Don't. Why do you keep hurting me, Faheem? Just answer me that. Why, my nigga? Why? Ain't I everything you said you wanted in a bitch?"

He reached for me again and this time pulled my ass into him when I resisted. He held me firmly in his arms and stared into my eyes. "Baby, that bitch is lying. Just like the last one. I got two babies out there and that's it. It's bad enough I've hurt you so much before, but I'm trying." He wiped my tears and kissed my lips. "I promise you. I'm not out here fuckin' around no more. That shits dead, Peyton. I promise you that. It's just me and you."

I wanted to believe him. I swear I did. I was so tired of giving him the benefit of the doubt. I was fed up with trying to make him see I was the one for him. I didn't know how much more bullshit I could take. He picked me up to place me on the counter and put my legs over his shoulders. That was just like Faheem to please me so good I'd forget the problem. But I never forgot. I just put it in the back of my mind for a while until the next situation arose. He was the problem, my problem. I just didn't know if or when I was going to solve it and how.

# SYNCERE

Rolling through the hood, I looked around, and I swear shit felt different. Eight years ago, there weren't corner boys hugging the block like they didn't have any sense. Bitches weren't walking around half naked with their hands out. Little kids were in camp or some shit. The cars were basic and less flashy. Man, the day I was released from Madison Correctional Institute, the hood was buzzing more than ever. Passing by my old stomping grounds, shit just seemed so unreal. A scene from New Jack City but the new era for real. I looked over at my cousin and wondered what type of shit he was into these days. The nigga was on some big time shit and I could tell. When I got locked up in 2012, niggas was only hustling weed and some E pills here and there. It was obvious from his clothes, car and jewels that this nigga was into way more than that shit.

"You good, nigga?" My cousin Teddy asked me.

I shrugged him off and nodded my head as my stomach started to growl. I was fucking starving. "Nigga, I'm tryna get some food. We been riding for a minute now. Where we going?"

"Relax, nigga. I got you. I'm finna run up in this spot real quick to grab something then we going to Church's, aight?"

I rubbed my hands together with a smirk on my face. "Yeah, hook it up!" For eight years, I'd been eating slop and although I knew the greasy Church's chicken would fuck my stomach up, I was all for it. A nigga was home now.

Teddy was really like a brother to me since his mother, my Aunt Jackie, took me in when my mother died after birth. This nigga was only two years older than me so we grew up close. I'll never forget the day I was in this nigga's car riding dolo one day just to go to the store to grab some chocolate cigarillos when I got pulled over. Bitch ass cops searched the car and found a loaded gun under the passenger seat, a couple knives, a loaded glock in the trunk and like three pounds of weed stashed all throughout his 2010 Honda Accord.

I couldn't believe the shit. They had me posted up on the side of the road straight embarrassed like I was a real criminal. Everybody knew me as Teddy's "lil' cousin", so folks was hanging around outside being nosey as shit. I'd never been locked up before prior to that. Teddy, being on his second strike at just twenty three, would have received crazy time in the pen. I took the wrap for that nigga and copped a plea for five to ten years in prison. I ended up serving eight long ass years while my cousin held my commissary down. He promised me he'd be there when I got out. I should have known by the last letter we exchanged that he was into some heavy shit now. He promised me he'd put me on to some major paper since he owed me one. I was twenty-nine now, and I made a mental note to see what was up with that promise as soon as I filled my empty stomach.

We pulled up to this bar that was clearly jumping from the long line outside and Teddy threw his white on white Bentley in park. "I gotta grab some shit, cuh." he told me. "I'mma be right back. Keep this bitch running."

He didn't even give me a chance to respond before he hopped out and disappeared into the bar. Some rough looking fools stood outside the joint eyeballing the whip like they wanted to run up. I rubbed my hands together and looked around my surroundings. I had an eerie feeling something bad was about to happen. I was praying this nigga Teddy hurried his business up before I had to fuck these niggas up.

*BANG! BANG! BANG! BANG!*

Shots rang out and the screams followed. Those niggas took off, the line of people outside the bar dispersed and a crowd of people flooded from the bar including Teddy's happy ass. He had blood all over his white tee and he ran to the whip carrying a big ass Louie duffle bag. He jumped in the car and tossed the bag in the back before screeching off around the corner.

"Nigga, what the fuck was that? That was you dumping in there?" I questioned loudly.

"Yeah, I had some business to tend to right quick."

"Bro, you said you was going to grab some shit, not shoot up some shit." I banged on the dashboard. "Fuck! You know a nigga just got out today, Teddy! The fuck is you doing?" I shook my head contemplating whether to jump out the moving car or keep riding.

"Aye, calm the fuck down, goddamn! I'll explain everything, my nigga. Geesh." Teddy pulled out his phone to make a call. "Yeah cuh, that's shits done, and I got the bag... you know that. I'mma get with you first thing in the a.m. I'm finna take my cousin to see some bitches!" He laughed into the phone and shoved me in the shoulder. "Aight. One hunnid." Teddy turned to me with a cheesy ass grin on his face as he sped through the hood. "See, everything's good. I got you." He reached into the glove compartment to pull at a fat ass blunt and handed it to me.

I hadn't smoked in eight years and truth be told, I wasn't that pressed to smoke weed again. But the way he cranked the music up and sparked the blunt told me to relax and enjoy the ride to

Church's. So, I did just that. Fuck it.

# CHAPTER TWO

# PEYTON

"Hey, mama. Good morning." I yawned into the phone before looking to my left and realizing I was sleeping alone. I closed my eyes and shook my head. Not only was I irritated that Faheem wasn't home, but it was Saturday and I planned on sleeping in. The clock on the nightstand read 7:45am. What could my mother possibly want this early?

"It's your father. He passed this morning, Pey." My mother sniffled into the phone. "My husband is gone, baby. He's gone," she sighed heavily.

I could feel her loneliness and grief through the phone. This was a day that we all knew was coming eventually but still, it was a hard pill to swallow. My dad was diagnosed with stage three kidney failure about eight months ago. With all the money and best doctors in the country, it still didn't matter. He was given six months to live so to see he strived to make it to eight months was a blessing in itself. My daddy, Calvin Jackson, was the best father ever and he was going to be missed like fucking crazy.

"Mama, I'm on my way, okay? Give me a few."

"Okay, baby," she sighed. "I have to call your

sister."

We hung up and I let out the biggest cry ever. I sat in the middle of the bed and cried for a few minutes before taking a several deeps breaths. My heart was racing.

"P, what's wrong? You alright?" I hadn't even heard Faheem come in our bedroom. I opened my eyes and he was standing right in front of me. He climbed onto the bed with a worried expression and pulled me close. "Talk to me. What's good, baby?"

I sniffed and sighed, "My daddy's finally gone. He passed this morning."

Now while Faheem and my dad barely got along when they were around each other, I knew he understood that this shit was killing me. This news just fucked me up. I grew up in a close-knit home with both parents and Paris. I was a daddy's girl to the fullest. He used to tell me I was like the son he never had because I loved shooting hoops with him on Saturdays and jogging with him on Sunday mornings. We'd have ice cream dates and attend daddy daughter luncheons while Paris and my mother shopped their asses off. Whenever you saw Calvin, you knew I wasn't too far behind. He didn't care for Faheem at all because of the life-style he lived and was disappointed in my choice of a man, but he didn't love me any less. My daddy was my first love and now he was gone forever.

Faheem held me tighter in his arms. "Damn, baby. I'm so sorry. Yo', whatever you need me to do, I got you." He cupped my face and kissed my lips. "Aight? I got you."

I nodded my head and replied, "Thank you, babe. Can you take me to my mom's? I don't think I should I drive right now."

"Whatever you need."

I got up, went into the bathroom to take a quick shower where I cried some more, then got dressed. I kept it simple throwing on some jeans, a tank top and Huaraches. My pixie cut was fresh, so I didn't have to worry about that part, and I hardly ever wore make up.

"You ready?" Faheem asked, standing in the doorway of the bathroom dressed in sweats and a white tee with some Jordan's. I gripped the edge of the sink and nodded my head 'yes'. He approached and reached for my hand. "I love you, Peyton. Know that."

We walked hand in hand through the crib to his 2020 cranberry Range Rover. I wanted to ask where he was all night, but I wasn't in the mood to hear the fabrications. I had to get to my mother.

\*\*\*

We drove about twenty minutes or so to Parkland and pulled up to the house that my parents shared their whole thirty-two years of marriage. The house was something out of a magazine and the illest on the street. Growing up, my sister and I were always hated on and the neighbors always poked their nose in our family business. Today was no different. It looked like a crime scene out front. Yellow caution tape wrapped around the entire front lawn, police surrounded the house, the fire department was there ready for whatever and a coroner. I guess I forgot to mention my daddy was a well-known police officer in Miami. Shit, from the looks of things, you would have thought the president himself died.

I turned to kiss Faheem before I got out of the car when I heard, "Mama, please come back in the house! Mama!" I recognized the voice as Paris' and immediately hopped out of the car.

"Shit..." My mother was attacking the coroner as he wheeled my daddy's dead body out of the house. Paris was doing everything she could to hold her back. "Mama, calm down!" I shouted as I held my hands up with my heart breaking.

"Mrs. Jackson, please... this is hard for all of us," a police officer said off in the distance.

"Fuck you!" My mother cursed as her tears steadily fell. She continued to struggle to get away from us and to my daddy. "Let me go, y'all. Please! I just wanna be with my Cal!" She cried out. Her movements became weaker and weaker. "Let me

23

go…that's my husband. That's…my…husband…"
My mother dropped to the ground crying hysterically and screaming, "Oh, Cal! Take me with you, baby! Lord, take me now!"

Paris and I cried with her in a huddle on the lawn. I hoped to never feel her pain. This was too much to bear. The police commissioner, Arnold, approached us with his hand over his heart and a pained looked upon his face. He said, "Mrs. Jackson…girls…you have my sincerest condolences." Tears welled up in his eyes as he spoke. "Calvin was a good man and a blessing to all of Miami. He will be deeply missed."

I sniffled and nodded my head then stood up to shake his head. "Thank you, Mr. Arnold." I gave a soft smile.

Paris rubbed our mother's back and helped her to sit on the steps, then turned her attention to Arnold. "We really appreciate you. Thank you for everything over the years." Paris wiped her tears.

Arnold continued, "If there's anything that any of you need, please let me or someone from the department know as soon as possible. His funeral expenses will be at no cost to your family. We'll take care of everything."

"Wow, that's really…" My words trailed off and my eyes zeroed in on Faheem giving this firefighter bitch googly eyes as he licked his lips. This fat bitch was all in his face as she leaned in the driver's side window grinning from ear to ear, twirling her fat ass fingers through her busted ass weave. The back of my neck became fiery hot, and I saw murder in my eyes. He never saw it coming.

"Aww come on, baby sister!" Paris called out to me. "Fuck that!"

Unfortunately, her words fell on deaf ears. Once again, Faheem had me all the way fucked up. I gripped the back of ol' girl's head and yanked her backwards. I two-pieced her real quick and gut punched her ass before she fell to the ground. "You muthafuckas got a lot of fuckin' nerve!"

Faheem jumped out of his car and snatched me off the firefighter as the officers ran over to us. "P, what the fuck, ma? Relax! Goddamn."

"Ms. Jackson, calm down!" Arnold shouted. "Oh, my! Jerrita, are you alright?"

The police and another firefighter brought their nosey asses over. I noticed some of the neighbors had gathered in the street to watch the fuckery as well. I knew it wasn't the time nor the place to act up like this but in that moment, I just couldn't control myself. My emotions were all over the place. Fuck him! Fuck everybody! I got super strength, broke free from Faheem's hold and slapped the color off his cheating ass, lying ass face.

"Are you serious right now? Of all times to wanna show some disrespect, huh? Are you fucking kidding me?!" I shoved him in his chest as tears clouded my vision.

"We were just fuckin' talking, little girl," Fat ass Jerrita chimed in as she dusted off her uniform and grilled me.

I started to approach her ass again. "Oh, bitch, you might wanna shut the fuck up..." Faheem snatched me back.

"Aye, cut the shit, Payton. For real, man."

"Get off me!"

"Okay, look, Ms. Jackson." Arnold held his hands out got serious. "I'm going to ask that you either calm down or leave the premises. Please, this isn't..."

"Leave?" I asked incredulously. "*I* have to leave? Nah, this is my daddy's house. This bitch can leave!" I lashed out. "Her services ain't even fucking needed." The look on my face told everyone to back off, and I wasn't playing. I turned to face Faheem who looked just as embarrassed as I felt. "Shit, you can leave too!" I cut my eyes at him and mumbled under my breath as I stormed off back towards the house.

"Oh, yeah? It's like that?" He yelled after me.

"Guess you don't need me then!"

"I guess I don't then!" I shook my head and kept walking past my mother and Paris I couldn't look at their faces. I knew they were both hurt, upset and embarrassed as shit. I'd just shown my natural crazy ass. I was sick of the blatant disrespect day in and day out. So fucking sick and tired. Man, something had to give.

# FAHEEM

I swear to God, Peyton was tripping as usual. I wasn't doing shit but talking to shorty on some real shit. Jerrita approached the car saying she was sorry for my loss and shit, so I told her thanks. Then of course she tried to slide some slick shit in the conversation by asking for my number and that's when Peyton came over acting a fucking fool. Baby girl went off and all I could do as I drove away from her parents' crib was shake my head.

I was a good nigga. Ever since I was a young one, I was taught to provide. That's what I was prone to do; take care of my family and nothing less than that. From the gate, eight years ago, I took care of Peyton. When we first met at the club, I knew exactly whose daughter she was. Calvin Jackson had been into politics most of my life, so I saw the man on TV, holding protest rallies in the hood and shit, trying to stop the violence. I was the exact opposite of who he wanted to be with his precious daughter and that made me want her ass even more. What could I really say? I was rebellious.

Peyton was freshly legal when I started fucking with her, so there was nothing nobody could really do about it. She wanted me, and I wanted her. Plain and simple. I put a ring on it after two years of just fucking around. I could tell she was really down for a nigga and despite her father's negative opinions, Peyton was glued to me. She was wife material and someone I could genuinely vibe with forever but I was still on some grimey shit back then. I mean, I had hella hoes all over Miami. She knew I had other bitches and seemed to be cool with it for the most part but soon enough, that changed. Most of these bitches were just a nut here and there, a few were reliable when it came to business and then the couple that I actually really fucked with I got stuck with. I wasn't trying to have no kids at all. Fuck that. I enjoyed the thrill of life too much to ever be locked down like that raising some kids.

I just knew Peyton was going to leave my ass after she found out about my son Junior almost six years ago, but that would be a lie. I could say I most definitely thought she was leaving my ass when she found out about my daughter Saraj three years ago, but that would be yet another lie. Truth is, she wasn't going anywhere at all. Big facts. I knew that, and she knew that. She loved me way more than I deserved, and her type of love was unconditional. My love for her ran deeper than the ocean. She was truly my other half. Our love was rare and there was no replacing that shit. No matter if I fucked around every once in a while, couldn't no bitch ever take Peyton's place.

A nigga had these streets on lock down and it had been that way for over a decade now. I been running things since I was eighteen and fresh out of high school and now I was thirty-two. I wasn't a dumb nigga by far. I had my Bachelor's Degree in Accounting, so fuck what you heard about trap niggas. We the shit. I managed to get my degree and pump the city with any drug you could think of. I was a solid nigga, if I did say so myself, with an even more solid team and production behind me. My brother, Saige and my good man's Teddy completed my main niggas and we all had a crew of young boys putting in the work. Trick Daddy could be the mayor of Miami, but I was the president and they were in my cabinet.

Pulling out my phone, I called up Teddy. Supposedly he had this cousin who got booked a few years back over some wild shit and now that the nigga was home, he asked me to put dude on with some work. I told him I'd meet him and see what was up, you know, feel him out or whatever. Regardless of the source, I wasn't about to just bring in any ol' body I didn't even know from a can of paint. My operation ran smoothly, and I didn't need any help.

"Yo, hold on real quick," Teddy answered and then the phone went dead for a few moments. He came back on the line and said, "What it do, cuh?"

"Ain't shit. What time you coning through with that?" I asked him, referring to the Louie bag full of heroin and money that he took back from this nigga Draco last night.

I'd been watching this nigga for a few weeks now. He was one of the young boys I employed and I found out he was getting extra product out of town to double his supply. Ultimately, he was plotting to build his own team over in North Lauderdale. I had no problems with a muthafucka trying to eat but not with my shit and definitely not behind my back in my muthafucking city. I was running shit, and I drew the line with the sneaky business. He had to work for his status just like I did. Fuck that. Being the king was no easy task and Draco saw firsthand what happened when you moved sneakily around me. I'd make sure his mother had what she needed for his burial.

"I got you," Teddy responded, bringing me back to the conversation at hand. "Gimme a few. I'mma go check on Nina 'cause she saying the twins ain't been feeling good and shit. After that, I'mma get with you."

"Aight, cuh. I'mma make my rounds," I informed him.

"Aye, real quick." He paused. "I was thinking of letting my cousin take these keys and see what he do with 'em."

I rubbed my chin and looked at the phone as if I'd heard him wrong. "Yeah? You boldly putting a lot on this nigga already."

Teddy laughed. "I told you, he my cousin. and he's a good nigga. On some real shit. Plus, I told him I'd look out for him when he touched down. Trust me, Heem, that nigga's good money," he told me.

I could hear the confidence and ego trip in his voice, but I said fuck it. I told him to set up a little meet and greet with his cousin at the Trillion House or the Trill as everyone called it. It was a poppin' ass nightclub where I conducted meetings from time to time. Plus, the buffet inside was always hitting, and I had a craving for that shit.

"Be there like around nine-thirty sharp, nigga." I reminded him. "I know how you get."

He laughed again. "Nigga, shut yo' ass up. I got you." We ended the call and I pulled up to Whitney's spot in Hillsboro. It was kind of a trip from where I stayed with Peyton but the two couldn't stand each other so I moved her ass further out.

It was a crisp Saturday morning and although I was slightly hungover and pissed at Peyton's shenanigans earlier, that wasn't going to stop me from shooting hoops with my son. Typically, we balled every Saturday morning and Junior loved every minute of it. He was waiting for me on the front porch. As soon as I beeped the horn, I watched him jump with excitement, open the door, yell something and then he took off running towards my car. He was tall to only be approaching six years old. He wanted to be the next Kobe, and I was there to see that shit happen. No funny shit, he was already nice on the court.

"Aye, pops." He greeted me with a hug.

"'Sup jit?" I kissed his forehead.

"Ugh, pops. That's gross." Junior frowned and wiped his forehead.

I laughed at his dramatics and replied, "Boy, where's yo' mama?" I looked over at the porch, expecting to see Whitney's salty ass come outside trying to fuck me per usual. Surprisingly, today she didn't. To be honest, she was just a "nothing else to do" type of fuck back in the day, and I should have been more careful with her ass. A nigga got caught slipping. Now while my son was no mistake by far, her ass most definitely was.

Junior shrugged his shoulders as he climbed into the back seat into his booster seat to buckle himself in. "I have no clue. When I woke up this morning, Ms. Claudine from across the yard was making pancakes. I guess she was watching me this morning, Pops."

I looked at the house then back at my son. "Yeah? Okay..." I started up the car and made a mental note to dig in Whitney's ass for having that old ass lady watching him. She was damn near ninety years old, blind in one eye and severely heard of hearing. Yeah, some explaining was needed.

# SYNCERE

"Girl, this nigga's dick is so big."

"And juicy. But bitch, next time share a lil' more. Yo' ass was all on it."

"Don't hate. I wonder what we getting today..."

I stirred out of my sleep and I thought a nigga was dreaming like I used to back in my days behind the wall. The feeling of soft hands rubbing all over my chest and thighs confirmed that this shit wasn't a dream at all. My eyes opened and I looked over to see a redbone chick grinning back at me while another light skin shorty beside me licked her lips. We were all naked on a big ass bed in a dope ass bedroom set up for a king to sleep in. Trap music played on the big ass flat screen Tv on the wall and my head my was already booming. There was weed, coke and some pills lying just chilling on the nightstand.

Looking at these bitches, I wondered who the fuck they were and where the hell I was at. "Excuse me, ladies but..."

Suddenly, the door burst open and in walked Teddy, fully clothed and banging a wooden spoon against a pot. "Aight bitches, it's time to go. Up and at 'em!" He started kicking the edge of the bed as the females got their naked asses up.

"Damn, it's like that? CoCo, fuck these niggas, girl." The tallest one shook her head as she tossed on her little red dress.

"Girl, what?" The short one looked at her friend like she was dumb as she began to get dressed as well. She slipped her pink dress on and mean mugged Teddy. "We rode here with y'all, remember? You can't ride us back to the hood?"

"Right. The least you could do is throw us some taxi fare or whatever."

"And what about the rest of the coke?"

I looked back and forth between all three of them, feeling hungover and lost as shit. What the fuck happened last night? Teddy threw the pot and spoon on the carpet then snatched both females up like they were some rag dolls.

"Bitch!" he barked. "Get the fuck outta here!" I quickly threw on my clothes. I heard them cussing his ass out and the front door open then slam. He made his way back to the bedroom singing, "'Cause we don't love these hoes. Aye, 'cause we don't love these hoes!"

I laughed. "Nigga, you wild." I plopped back

down on the bed and said, "Yo, what the fuck did we do last night, bro?" I asked, this time aloud.

Sparking up a blunt, he replied, "Nah, nigga. The question is, what did *you* do last night?" He held out the blunt for me to hit. "Shake that shit off."

I waved him off. "Man, I'm good. All I remember is fucking up some Church's and smoking mad blunts with yo' ass." I held my head in my hands. My shit was rocking!

Teddy puffed on the blunt and with the mouth full of smoke said, "Nigga, that's what coke and weed will do to you. Have yo' ass gone." When he said that shit, I shot to my feet and walked up on my cousin like he was some nigga off the street.

"Fuck you just say, cuh?" I towered over his frame. "I ain't no fucking fiend! Fuck is you talking 'bout?" I balled up my fists and bit down on my bottom lip. I was ready to knock this nigga the fuck out. He had me too hot that I almost forgot that he was my blood for a quick second.

Teddy held the blunt on the tip of his mouth and put his hands up. He responded, "Relax, nigga. My bad. I just figured since you were fresh out, you could use a good ass night. No funny shit, bro."

I gritted my teeth and eyeballed this nigga up and down. He was still my cousin, my bro, my nigga, but he had me fucked up right now. That was some funny ass shit to pull regardless of the situation. "Nigga, if that's what you do then do you. Don't put me on to that shit, aight? Final warning, my nigga. I ain't with that shit. You know that. I'll roll up my own shit from now on, feel me?" I told him.

He laughed and nodded his head. "Aight, nigga. We good?"

I nodded my head back and made my way out of the bedroom into the living room. I couldn't front; the crib was dope. I'm talking laid the fuck out. I could tell a female handled the decor because Teddy wasn't the type.

"Whose crib is this anyway?"

"Oh, this is one of my old spots I used to keep some shit in. But now-" His cell phone rang, and he cut the conversation short. He answered. "Hold on, bro." He reached into his jeans and pulled out a knot of money along with a set of house and car keys. Handing them to me, he said, "Here, that's you, cuh. This yo' spot now until you get on yo' feet and move on up like a real nigga." He laughed and popped the color on his crisp ass shirt. "Take that bread and you know, get fresh nigga. You home now. You can push that Altima out front for now too." He dapped me up and pulled me in for a bro hug. "I'mma get with you a lil' later. Get a phone too, nigga and text the number I left in the glove compartment, aight?

Be easy." He went back to the phone conversation and left the crib before I had the chance to question shit.

Looking at the wad of money in my hand and the keys, I raised my eyebrow thinking two things; Teddy was definitely into some heavy shit and how the fuck could I get down. Simple as that. I ain't never relied on a single soul to put money in my pockets, so this shit was fucking with me a little bit. But he kept his word and so far, he was looking out for a nigga. I was grateful but whatever my cousin was on, I was trying to be on with too ASAP! I proceeded to get ready for the day.

\*\*\*

Carol City is where I grew up at so to be living back in the same area made me feel comfortable but none of the old faces were around. That told me niggas were either dead or in jail. I breathed in the fresh late August air as I stood outside taking in my surroundings. I had taken a hot ass shower and tossed on the same dusty clothes I wore yesterday when I was released. The first stop was the barbershop and then hit up the shopping center. I was about to go crazy, shit, Syncere was back in the hood muthafuckas! I had to get on my shit.

I cruised down the street bumping the radio. Pulling up to a red light, I bopped my head to Roddy Rich's *The Box* and watched as this slim thick, brown skin shorty stepped into the crosswalk. I licked my lips. She was fine as fuck. Not wearing anything too impressive, just some jeans and fresh kicks, there was something about her walk that intrigued me. The wave of her hips and the arch in her back had me stuck. Her haircut was dope too with the undercut design, and I didn't even like bald chicks. Although she rocked a mean mug, she was a sight for sore eyes.

I couldn't help but to say something, so I rolled down the window and slightly leaned out. "Smile beautiful!" I called out. "Tomorrow will be a better day."

She made it over to the car where another female was waiting in the driver's side and turned to look back at me with her face even more screwed up. Cars honked behind me. I winked at her and turned the corner, making sure to get a good look at her one more time. I'd see her again. That was a big fact.

# CHAPTER THREE

# PEYTON

"Girl, who was that fine ass nigga hollering at you?" Milah asked me with a cheesy ass grin on her face when I hopped back in her car.

After the shit show outside my parents' house, I had to ask her to come get me since I told Faheem to leave. Of course, my mother grilled my ass and Paris cussed me out for acting a fool, but their words fell on deaf ears. Nobody really knew all of the bullshit I endured with him simply because I didn't "runteldat" every time there was a problem. They knew enough though, hence, why they both lashed out at me. Now Milah being my best friend, well, shit, she knew all the nitty gritty. I gave her ass a blank stare and just shrugged my shoulders.

"Milah, I don't know every nigga in Miami like your ass. I'm surprised you don't know who he was," I chuckled. "Besides, he looked too raggedy to even be tryna holla at somebody like me especially driving that damn Altima. I'm spoken for and my daddy just died." I reminded her and let out a deep, sad ass sigh as the tears threatened to fall again. I sucked them up and continue. "Ain't nobody thinking about shit that is irrelevant. Sorry not sorry."

Milah peeled her Mercedes away from the curb and into the flow of traffic. "I know, P. You know I was just fucking with you. Look, I say we do something tonight." I started to protest but she cut me off. "Uh uh, hear me out. I think you need to let loose and take your mind off some things, even if it's just for the moment."

"Something like what?" I turned my nose up as I received a text from Paris telling me that I need to do better and realize what's important in life. I put my phone on "Do Not Disturb" and dropped it back in my lap. "Millz, you know I don't do the clubs like that." I gave her the side eye.

"Club?" She laughed. "Girl, ain't nobody talking 'bout no ratchet ass club. Dang. I was thinking a little girls' night out for some food and drinks. We can talk shit and get lit." She stuck her tongue out at me. "You know we still ain't try that new seafood spot down on the boulevard." She licked her lips. "Mmmm, mmm, mmm..."

I couldn't help but laugh at her greedy ass because Milah Ballard was a fat ass bitch in a slim chick's body! There was no doubt about that. Home girl could eat. But seeing as though there were renovations being done to my stores this weekend, I really didn't have much to do to occupy my time, and I definitely didn't want to be up under Faheem ass for the night. I decided to take my best friend up on her offer and told her the night was on her. Seafood and drinks were my favorite.

I was going to treat myself. Fuck it, why not? I worked hard. See, I was more than just Faheem's "lil' fiancé". I was a boss chick. I owned three boutiques in the city of Miami. Cashmere was for the club nights when you wanted something tight and right to make a nigga want to spend some bread. Youth Lot was for the kids and young adults. There you could find the hottest trends and the most exclusive kicks. And finally, my last boutique was Radiance. This store was a big money maker around prom and for weddings. Also, the average workingwoman could find the best blouses and skirts to step into the office with.

I was an entrepreneur at her peak and to top it all off, Faheem didn't control shit because I didn't use his money to start none of it. My daddy invested in my dream and it was definitely paying off. I had my own money and independence. I planned on opening a fourth boutique that was strictly for the fellas, but I was still unsure of my plan and the layout. I had goals. I needed to remember that and stop putting so much energy into the bullshit.

Milah and I grabbed some quick food and by the time she dropped me back off at home, emotionally I was drained and physically, I was exhausted. I needed a nap and being that I knew

Faheem would be gone for a few hours with Junior, I planned to do just that.

***

*"And darling, I will be loving you 'til we're 70 and baby, my heart could still fall as hard at 23. And I'm thinking 'bout how people fall in love in mysterious ways. Maybe just the touch of a hand. Oh, me I fall in love with you every single day and I just wanna tell you I am..."*

*"And do you, Peyton Nicole Jackson, take this man to be your lawfully wedded husband until the day you both shall live?"*

*I looked up at Faheem with a bright smile and he was staring back with tears in his eyes. I just knew this was it. The moment I'd been fighting for since the beginning of time. I was finally going to be Mrs. Shamir! My lips parted to utter the words "I do" when someone shouted out. "You can't marry him, P! I love you. Marry me!"*

I immediately jumped out of my slumber, panting hard as hell with my heart beating a mile a minute. I was breathing like a fat bitch walking up the stairs. Damn near everybody I knew called me P but I didn't recognize the voice or see a face. That shit was creepy as fuck.

"What the hell?" I wondered as I looked around the bedroom. Then, I frowned when I noticed a pair of Jordan's by the foot of the bed, which let me know Faheem was home.

I was knocked. It was almost seven in the evening. I slept most of this sad ass day away and woke up to several missed calls and texts. Some were from Milah and then of course Faheem saying he was sorry per usual, he loved me, and he'd made us dinner reservations for eight o'clock at my favorite restaurant by the water. I exited his message thread to text Milah back to see what was up with our plans for the evening. That was just like this nigga, thinking the sun rose and set on his ass like I didn't have shit to do.

"Sleepyhead…" He kissed the back of my head and walked by smelling like a God. He was wrapped in a plush towel dripping wet. "'Bout time you woke up. We gon' be late for dinner." I had to peel my eyes away from his sexy ass. He would not get me this time. I cleared my throat and threw my phone on the bed before replying.

"I got plans with Milah tonight, Heem." I climbed off the bed and took my earrings off. We made eye contact. "Sorry."

He dropped his towel to the carpet and began to oil his body down. My pussy tingled. I had to tell that bitch to calm the fuck down! He nodded his head and continued to stare me down as he said, "Is that right? Where you think y'all going?"

I blatantly rolled my eyes and replied, "Out for drinks. I had a bad morning, if you recall, and I'm tryna have a better night."

Faheem walked over to me, long dick swinging and wrapped his arms firmly around my waist. Licking his lips, he asked, "You think you gon' leave me by my lonesome tonight?" He kissed my neck passionately, and I shivered. "Huh?"

*Nah, Peyton! Get it together, bitch. You're still mad! Bitch, be mad!* I squirmed to free myself, but it wasn't happening; he just held me tighter. I looked up at him and his look was deadly. "You leave me alone every night, baby," I sarcastically told him and felt his grip loosen. "Let's see how you like waking up alone." I cut my eyes at him and pushed away from him.

He snatched me back with the quickness. "You thought that shit was funny, P?"

"Did you hear me laugh, Heem?" I shot back.

We stared each other down, neither of us giving in. He applied pressure to my arm. Faheem never hit me before, so I wasn't worried about that, but something in the way he stared at me made me question it right then. I knew he could be a cold ass nigga when pushed to that point. I swallowed hard as he let my arm go and turned his back to me.

He spoke coldly as he said, "Enjoy yo' night

and be home in my bed before I get home."

His tone of voice placed a little fear in my heart as I grabbed my phone off the bed and slowly backed out of the bedroom. Once in the bathroom, I turned the shower on and thought back to what Milah said. I just has to let loose and enjoy the night.

# SYNCERE

A nigga like me ain't never been to a club before. It probably sounded crazy but it was the truth. Before I got locked up all those years ago, I was only twenty-one and heavily into the hood. I fucked bitches and sold bud. That was it. I wasn't too into turning up in clubs and shit like some niggas but tonight, I was gon' step out.

After getting a fresh cut, I tore the mall down. Teddy gave me a few stacks, but I wasn't stupid enough to blow it all. I definitely bought me some fly shit though to get me through until this nigga put me on with his peoples. He mentioned going to Club Trill for a lil' meet and greet with his homie. He went by the name of Faheem and apparently the nigga was hot shit out in Miami, moving all types of shit. I wanted a piece of it all. I could taste the smell of new money and I was ready for it.

Leaving out the mall, I felt my ribs touching. A nigga was starving like Marvin and craving soul food like a muthafucka, so I drove all the way across town to The Licking for some good ol' down home cooking. I ordered fried catfish, collard greens, mac and cheese, yams and some cornbread with an extra large sweet tea. I rubbed my belly with anticipation of busting this food down. I wasn't a small nigga by far. A nigga was big and handsome. I stood six feet four inches tall and weighed about two-ninety-five last I checked. I'd always been a big nigga and bitches loved me for that on top of my clear, brown skin and deep waves. I rubbed my hands over my fresh cut, glad to be back to normal.

As I stood in line waiting for my food, I felt a tap on my shoulder. I wasn't too fond of people I didn't know touching me, so I turned around with my face screwed up, wondering who the fuck was bold enough to touch me.

"Well, daaaaamn, Syncere. It's nice to see you again too."

It was Kida, a petite red bone with deep dimples and a heart of gold. We used to fuck around off and on back in the day before I got bagged. I wouldn't have called her my girl or anything, but we were doing our thing or whatever for an ill minute. She would ride with me to bust some plays and would sneak me in her crib when her mama was too high to pay attention. I would do the same when my aunt worked some overnight shifts.

Kida was cool peoples. She wrote me a few times while I was locked up and came to visit me a time or two in the beginning years. I looked her up and down and noticed she'd gained weight but in a good way. She looked good as fuck, but I was hesitant on rekindling with her. She was low key ratchet as hell with little ambition. Plus, what we had in the past was on some teenybopper type shit. I could have honestly dismissed her right then and there, but I chose to not be a dick head. I cracked a light smile and pulled her in for a tight hug.

"What's going on, Kida?"

She flipped her long, curly hair over her shoulders and smirked up at me. "Well, you know me, baby. Same ol' same. How about I buy you lunch, and we can uh..." She caressed my cheek softly. "Catch up?"

I licked my lips and entertained the thought of fucking with her. It was still hella early, so I had time to kill until this little meet and greet at the club later. I took her up on her offer but paid for both of our meals instead. She wasn't about to buy me a muthafucking thing with the next nigga's money.

About an hour later, I had Kida bent over the marble countertop in the kitchen moaning her ass off. I wasn't dumb, a nigga strapped up but her pussy was still fire. I couldn't resist the temptation once we finished our food and light conversation over some trap music. I slapped her juicy ass and gripped her hair as I plunged deeper inside of her.

"Damn, Kida…" I groaned. She threw her ass back at me and looked back. She tightened her pussy muscles at the same time I felt my grip slipping on her hair.

"Uh huh. This pussy feels bomb, don't it? You miss me or nah?"

I couldn't even front, I did miss her ass a lil' bit so I said, "Hell yeah." Lifting one of her legs up in the crook of my arm, I bent down so I could go even deeper. Kida gripped the countertop and bit her bottom lip.

"Shit, Syncere. Goddamn…" she whined as her eyes rolled in the back of her head.

I smirked as I regained control of this fuck session. "Uh huh, take all this dick." I hit her with the left death stroke as she came for the second time. I could feel myself about to bust a big ass nut my damn self. I dropped her leg and gripped her tiny waist then quickened my pace. Sweat dripped onto the small of her perfectly arched back. Kida screamed out in pleasure and started moaning like crazy.

"Yessss! Tear this pussy up, baby. Fuck!"

"Shit, I'm 'bouta nut too." I held her firmly by her waistline then pulled out. Without hesitation, Kida turned around and sucked every last drop of cum from my dick, then she circled the head with her tongue ring and proceeded to make me bust yet another wild ass nut. My legs trembled on some crazy shit. She smiled up at me as she licked her lips. I caressed her cheek. I don't know what came over me but I definitely asked her ass to kick it with me for the rest of the weekend.

# FAHEEM

Peyton knew like I knew that her ass better be in the crib before I got back home so I wasn't tripping. I knew she had a rough morning so fuck it, I allowed her to go out. She got dressed in the guest bedroom in a long-sleeved nude dress with wedges and big gold hoops looking good as fuck. She wore a deep burgundy lipstick, grabbed her clutch and left the crib leaving her fragrance lingering behind. I couldn't even front; my bitch was bad as fuck. For a moment, I questioned whether she was going to meet up with Milah for real or another nigga. I laughed out loud at the thought and shrugged that shit off.

"Yeah, aight. She knows who daddy is." I slid my Rollie on and adjusted the sleeve on my rose gold collared shirt. See, the thing about me, I may have been a thug, trap god, drug lord and whatever else the Feds would consider me, but I never dressed the part. I always dressed to impress unless I was just coolin' out, kicking it, then I'd be dressed down in some jeans or sweats and sneakers. I slipped into my Tom Ford loafers and it felt like a nigga floated to the other side of the room to answer my ringing phone. I crackled a soft smile as I answered.

"Yeah, hello?"

"Hey love," my homegirl, Lala, purred into the phone. "You on your way to scoop me?"

I checked the time on my watch to see that I was right on schedule. I tucked my glock and then tossed on my blazer. I responded, "Yes, ma'am. I'mma be to you in like fifteen, aight?"

"Mmmm..." she moaned. "I'll definitely be waiting."

What was dinner and healthy conversation with a friend? Peyton pissed me off when a nigga was really out here trying to be on his best behavior lately. So, I did what I wanted to do which was treat Lala to a nice lobster dinner and wine then I let her suck me into relaxation in the back seat of my Rover. I handed her some dough to take a taxi to wherever she was going next, cleaned my dick off, then made my way to The Trill. Lala knew what time it was whenever we linked up which is why I always liked fucking with her. I could always count on her to keep it just between us whereas some of these bitches out here felt the need to bump they lips, telling the whole city they done had this golden dick. What Peyton didn't know couldn't hurt her.

\*\*\*

*"She like the way that I dance, she like the way that I move. She like the way I rock, she like the way I*

*woo...*" I pulled up to the front of the club bumping the late Pop Smoke and told the nigga out front not to scratch my shit. It was about ten o'clock when I finally got there. Yeah, I know I told this nigga Teddy to be there a half an hour before, but I had my reasons. Fuck a line and VIP. I walked right up to the front door like I owned the bitch.

"Oh, shit. What it do, Heem?" The bouncer, Joe, dapped me up. "Ain't seen you up in here in a good lil' minute."

I popped my collar a little bit and looked back at some bitches drooling over me. I turned back to Joe and replied, "Yeah, well, you know where I be, cuh." I slipped him a hundred-dollar bill. "Yo, you seen my brother come through here?"

"Yup, he went on up to the second floor," Joe responded to me.

"Aight, good looks, Joe. I'mma get with you." I dapped him up again. Choosing to avoid the crown, I kept it pushing and opted to take the emergency stairwell by the front entrance. I gave Teddy instructions to meet me in VIP on the lower level, but I didn't plan on being there. I had Saige get some information on this nigga Teddy's cousin and their family history prior to meeting me at the club.

I cracked the conference room door open

and greeted my brother with a bro hug. He ashed his blunt and said, "Damn, nigga. Got me in here babysitting niggas on camera and shit," he laughed.

"Nigga, shut up." I snatched the blunt from him. Saige and I were only eleven months apart on some Irish twins type shit, but I was the older one, so I punked his ass sometimes. Don't get it twisted though, my brother was just as much of a God as I was. People often mistook us for twins except he was light skin and kept his hair low. He was about the same height with a slim build as well. I was the rational thinker whereas this nigga Saige never hesitated to do some wild shit. Nigga's didn't call him Savage for a reason. I nodded my head towards the cameras on the wall in front of us. "What's good with this nigga?" I asked, referring to Teddy's cousin then hit the blunt. My brother began to break shit down.

"Aight, so peep. His name is Syncere Anthony King, age twenty-nine, no parents, no siblings, no kids, and he just came home from an eight-year bid." I raised my eyebrow at that. He continued, "Drugs and gun charges on some crazy shit. And get this shit, the car he got booked in back then was registered to a Theodore Lewis Stephens. He had two priors at the time." My brother handed me a manila folder, and we locked eyes.

"Say word?" I skimmed through the investigation packet he handed me and rubbed my chin. "Okay, okay. So, he took the wrap for Teddy to avoid this nigga doing some crazy time, huh?" I assumed but it was evident that's exactly what happened. "That's a ride or die cousin right there." I laughed. "Nigga took one for the team at an early age." I hit the blunt again and passed it back to my brother.

"Uh huh..." Saige nodded his head and inhaled the weed. "He definitely did. Eight years. But, so what? The question is, can you trust him to do the same if or when shit ever hits the fan? Teddy and him grew up as close as brothers all their lives 'til that shit happened and even then, didn't he tell you he was holding him down while locked up?"

"Yeah, that's what he said."

"We ain't blood. He don't owe you shit, and I'll be quick to put a bullet through his skull if shit goes sideways," Saige spoke matter-of-factly.

I laughed. "Nigga, relax. Lemme feel his ass out first. I know Teddy wouldn't vouch for no lame ass nigga." I turned to the cameras and watched as some bitches danced on him while Syncere sat back with a thick, red bone planted on his lap. They were hugged up so I assumed it was his shorty. I'd have to school him on that shit; never bring sand to the beach. He seemed like the laid back type as he vibed to the music and chugged from the D'Ussé bottle. Me and my brother finished the blunt and got ready to head downstairs. "Come on, nigga. Let's pop out on these niggas."

When we approached VIP, Teddy was so caught up entertaining the hoes that he didn't even peep we had arrived until one of the shorties exclaimed, "Oh shit, bitch. It's Heem!"

"What up, cuh?" Teddy slurred his words and greeted us. "'Bout time you blessed the spot with yo' presence. Aye, ladies, give us a minute, aight?" He slapped both the chicks' asses as they exited VIP. "Goddamn..." He cocked his head to the side.

I dapped him up and said, "You know a nigga always handling business."

"What's good?" Saige gave him a bro hug as well and reached for a D'Ussé bottle from the ice box in the middle of the table.

"Yo, cuh," Teddy tapped his cousin's shoulder. "These is my bros, Heem and Savage. Y'all, this my cousin, Syncere. He a good nigga. I'm tryna tell yo' ass." He was all grinning and shit like a proud father.

I dapped him up with a handshake while Saige nodded his head and said, "What it do?" Neither of us acknowledged his shorty.

"Shit, cuh," Syncere responded. "A nigga just glad to be home, feel me?" He adjusted his fitted and made eye contact with me. "I hear you the man with the master plan who got the game inside his hand. I'm tryna see what's good with that, big dawg." He turned the bottle up and took a swig.

I liked a person who got straight to the point and left very little to be uncertain about. But on the downside, I didn't like to be rushed into conversation either. This nigga would find that out. I went to reply, and his shorty cut me right off. Rolling her neck, she popped her lips.

"Um, well since everyone wanna act like I'm just not even sitting here, allow me to introduce myself." She cut her eyes at Syncere and slid off his lap. She pulled her tight ass dress down and batted her eyelashes up at me with an extended hand. "What's good, Heem? I'm Kida. It's nice to meet you. I, uh, hope you can put my man here onto some real paper, feel me?" She winked at me with a wide grin.

I heard Teddy mumble, "Aw shit..." He shook his head. Saige sat up on the couch with his arms folded, looking dumbfounded. I know he was thinking the same shit I was thinking. This bitch was bold as fuck. She was eye fucking the shit out of me right in front of her own nigga. I looked past her to see Syncere grilling the fuck out of her ass and if looks could have killed, this bitch would have been six feet under in that exact moment.

He jaw flexed as he gripped her by the elbow to pull her close. "Lemme holla at this man real quick, aight?" He reached in his pockets then handed her a crisp hundred-dollar bill. "Go wait for me by the bar next to the elevators." They made brief eye contact then Kida kissed his cheek and left VIP with the money. I could tell this nigga was embarrassed.

"She a lil' ratchet, cuh," Saige chimed in.

I took a seat beside my brother on the couch and poured me up a glass of D'Ussé. Laughing a little bit, I asked Syncere, "That's yo' girl?"

"Nigga, Kida a lil' hoe!" Teddy stood up and stumbled a little bit. "I'm surprised you don't know her slime ass. This nigga crazy for that one."

"Nah," I quickly shook my head and rubbed my beard. "You know the caliber of bitches I fuck with. First off, my bitch ain't gon' be up in the club with me anyway. Some shit pop off, it's a wrap for niggas." I made sure to make eye contact with Syncere when I said, "You'll get to know the game."

He nodded and rubbed his hands together then replied, "I feel that but my shorty go wherever I go comfortably because she gon' always know I'm her protector through whatever."

I cracked a light smile, looked over at my brother who was staring back at me, then I turned to face Teddy. "Where you find this man, cuh? Nigga got heart like a muthafucka."

We all shared a quick laugh and then got down to business. I could tell Syncere was trying to prove himself in the presence of a boss ass nigga, but it wasn't necessary. I'd made up my mind that I'd let him take the three keys from Teddy as a start off. I liked his cousin's energy and the fact that he did a bid for my nigga spoke volumes. Real nigga shit. I took that as he wasn't afraid to take risks and do the time if necessary. I needed muthafuckas like that around. As we conversed, I got the notion Syncere was level-headed and a smooth talker just trying to get on his feet. I could respect anybody looking to better their current situation. I made a mental note to have a separate conversation with this nigga Teddy about some shit but for now, his cousin was down.

"Welcome home, cuh." I raised my glass and we all toasted to some exclusive shit.

# PEYTON

The day I watched my daddy lay stiff in a satin coffin will forever be burned in my mind. In the front pew of Grace Baptist Church, I held my mother in my arms while Paris clutched her shaking hand. I listened as Miami PD, the governor, close friends and family spoke about my dad's life. WPLG Local 10 news went live during the entire funeral. Calvin Jackson was a great man and the epitome of what a leader is. My daddy never had enemies and always did the right things in life.

Paris and I went up to the podium with my mother in front of the closed casket when it was our time to speak. The sadness, pain and loneliness in her voice echoed throughout the church as she spoke about early life with Calvin and raising us. My mother thanked the city of Miami for always being there in support of our family. Paris shared a few words through a tearful speech then the moment came for me to speak, and I froze up like a deer in headlights.

It was like my life flashed before my eyes. I could smell the hospital room and hear my little cries. I felt the discomfort of my first tooth growing in. I could feel the burn on my left knee as I scraped it across the pavement when I fell off my shimmery gold bike. I heard my daddy telling me when somebody hits me to hit them back when I got suspended from middle school for fighting in the cafeteria. I could still feel his arms around me when he hugged me outside the house before I left for prom night. I tasted the Southern Comfort on my tongue when he poured me up a drink the day I found out about Faheem's first child. I could still hear his heartbeat as I laid my head on his chest a few short weeks ago.

I started hyperventilating as I looked around at everyone staring at me waiting for me to speak. My vision then became blurry and my top lip started sweating. My whole left side went numb. I felt a sharp pain attack my abdomen as warm liquid trickled down my legs, ruining my brown suede pumps. Out of nowhere, my entire body became weak and I tumbled down the steps and fell right next to my daddy's casket damn near knocking it over. I heard screams and gasps. My eyes rolled in the back of my head. I was out.

\*\*\*

*Beep...beep...beep...beep...*

My eyes fluttered open and I glanced around wondering how the hell I ended up in a hospital. At my bedside sleeping uncomfortably in a chair was Faheem with his hand rested softly on my stomach. My vision was foggy, and I had the worst cramps ever. I looked around to see Paris on the other side of the room slumped in a chair with my mother's head in her lap. Milah sat beside them with her mouth open, snoring her ass off.

"What the fuck?" I spoke softly. The last thing I could remember was getting ready for my daddy's funeral. Now here I was, laid up in the same hospital he spent his last few weeks in. This shit was wild. I reached for Faheem's hand and tried to speak but my mouth was dry as shit, so I just cleared my throat as loud as I could.

He stirred out of his sleep and quickly jumped up. His eyes were bloodshot and puffy as if he'd been crying for days. He bent down to kiss my lips and whispered, "'Sup, baby?" He looked up and said, "Aye y'all, she's awake. P's up, y'all." Everyone began to wake up as he cried out to me. "Baby, I'm sorry. I'm so sorry." Tears welled up in his eyes when he touched my belly. "I swear to God, I'm so sorry, baby."

"What?" I coughed, sounding all confused. Finding my voice, I asked, "What are you talking about? What's going on?" Then it dawned on me that he was apologizing for not being able to make to my daddy's funeral. I patted his hand to reassure him that it was fine. "Don't cry, babe. I mean, it's alright. It's okay."

"Oh, Peyton!" My mother collapsed on top of me. "I can't take no more death, Lord Jesus. Fix it now! Bless her!" She hollered.

"Ma, calm down." Paris lifted her up to comfort her. "I'm going to get the doctor, nurse...shit, somebody." She hurriedly left the room.

"Will somebody please tell me what the hell is going on?" I tried to make eye contact with somebody...anybody. They were starting to scare the shit out of me. I looked up at Faheem who just stared back at me. "Why am I here? What happened? Why is everyone tripping?" I bombarded him with questions.

Milah held my mother in her arms as she broke down. "Ma, it's going to be alright." She looked at me with a somber look and gave a soft smile. "It's gon' be just fine, best friend. I promise you."

I tried to sit up when a sharp pain hit my side. "Ugh, what the fuck?" I groaned. I could something wasn't right. Just when I was about to flip the fuck out, the room door swung open and in walked Paris with a doctor holding a medical chart.

"Ms. Jackson," she greeted me with a pained look plastered on her face. "So happy that you're awake."

"Listen, doc, fuck the small talk please." I begged her. "What is going on? Tell me something since they won't. Please. Why am I here? I have to make it to my daddy's funeral."

"Oh, Cal!" My mother cried out yet again. She was a hysterical mess. "I can't take this. I cannot do this!" She gathered up her belongings and bolted out of the room. Faheem gripped my hand as rubbed his watery eyes as the doctor spoke.

"Peyton, I need you to try to remain calm, honey." She sighed. "You suffered a serious concussion three days ago at your father's funeral and..."

"Three days ago?!" My head was spinning. Everyone stood around in silence waiting for the doctor to finish speaking.

"Yes. You had a severe panic attack as well as..." She glanced around the room at my friend and family then lastly, at my man.

"Just spit it out, doc. Please!"

"Well, you also suffered a very bad miscarriage. The baby was nine weeks and there was nothing we could do to save it." She wiped her eyes as a tear threatened to fall. "You have my sincerest apologies."

"Wait, what?! Nah..." I violently shook my head. "A miscarriage? No...no...no..." the tears flowed like a river. "You're lying!"

"Baby, it's true." Faheem confirmed the worst news ever as he choked back tears. "I'm so sorry, ma." I clawed at my stomach.

"This isn't real. This isn't happening right

now. Yeah, that's right. This is just a bad dream." I tried to convince myself, nodding my head. "One fucked up ass nightmare. That's all. That's all." I closed my eyes tightly.

"Baby sister," Paris called out to me with tears in her eyes. "If I could trade places with you, I would in a fuckin' heartbeat. I swear to God."

I shook my head and looked over at Milah. "Millz, this isn't real, right? Please tell me she's lying...please. Please, please..." I begged.

Milah cried and shook her head 'no' before replying, "I'd never seen so much blood, P. I thought..."

"Don't say that!" The doctor snapped at her.

At that point, I lost it. I screamed so loudly, everyone jumped. "Oh, my God! No! Why me Lord? Why?!" First my daddy and now my first child was gone. How? Why? What did I do to deserve this tragedy? Bitches poppin' up on doorsteps with babies and calling my phone with babies, yet the Lord took mine from me. Why God? Why? I started flipping the fuck out in that hospital room. "Everybody leave me the fuck alone! Get out! Get the fuck out now! Right now! Get the fuck out!" I held my belly and curled up as best as I could. "Oh, my God! Why? Get out! Get the fuck out!" I shouted over and over again.

I heard the doctor say, "She's in shock. I've

seen situations like this go from bad to worse so please, I think it's best that you all leave at this time. Please give her some space."

"On some real shit, doc, I ain't leaving," Faheem protested.

"You're probably the reason this shit even happened. Got me stressed the fuck out over you and these bitches!" I reached out to slap him, but I missed. Another sharp pain attacked my body and I winced in pain. "Urgh! Get the fuck out!!! I fuckin' hate you! I hate you! I hate you..." I cried and cried and cried. I wouldn't have wished this pain on my worst fucking enemy.

# CHAPTER FOUR

TWO MONTHS LATER

# SYNCERE

"Why can't you return a phone call or a text message,? What, you good on me or something? What, you got another bitch or something? Huh? Is that it? Nah, wait, I know just what it is. You think you too good to fuck with lil' ol' me these days, huh? You think you special now? You think you better than somebody? Tuh! Nigga, I don't need you. I never did! Shit, the same way you came up is the same fucking way you can get knocked back down, muthafucka! Be humble. You need a bitch like me and you'll realize that shit when it's too fucking late, okay! Nigga, fuck you!" *CLICK!*

I laughed and shook my head as I listened to Kida's umpteenth voicemail. Shorty was bugging out for real. I sat on the edge of my bed and slipped in my customized cherry wood Timbs. Wintertime was approaching and although it was like seventy degrees outside, I was still gon' rock my Timbs faithfully. That was just my style. My phone chimed, alerting me that I had received a text and I was more than sure it was from Kida. Sure enough, it was her ass again. The text read:

*KIDA: Damn, so you really ain't fucking with me no more? Like, on some real shit? Why Syncere?*

*What did I do to you? Ugh…call me.*

I tossed my phone back onto the bed, brushed my waves and said to myself, "Yo', she's really crazy. Damn." One minute she was rashing my life then the next she sounded all sweet as candy. Either way, I was all set.

Shaking my head, I reflected on the last several weeks. Literally, two months ago I reeked of prison tiles and hand me downs, wondering if or when I was going to come up. Now today, I was standing in my own crib with a safe full of jewels and my own money. I had to give it to Teddy props because he kept his word and really looked out for a nigga by putting me on with this nigga Heem. I got those three kilos of coke off in less than a week. He was impressed by my work ethic and put me to the test. He took his cut, threw me mine, then handed me five keys and told me move the shit in less than a week. On my solo dolo shit, you would have thought I sold hard drugs prior to this the way I moved. I was so smooth, and niggas loved Heem's product, which made shit even easier. I brought the man back his cut in four days.

This nigga joked that if I kept moving shit so swiftly, I would be taking his job. See, that wasn't my plan at all though, and I didn't necessarily want to sell drugs forever. All I wanted was a spot of my own, a new whip, fresh clothes and money stacking up. In the joint, I dreamed of opening a clothing store or some exclusive shit. Every nigga sold drugs and went to jail, but I thought I wanted to do something different.

Shit, after like a month and a half of selling cocaine, man...all that "different" shit went out the window. I was touching more paper than I'd ever seen in my twenty-nine years of existence. I wasn't too happy I didn't have a team of my own yet but for the mean time, I was the over-seer of Heem's young boys. Shit was lovely. As long as the product moved, the money flowed like a river. Everything was going smoothly outside of the fact that I caught a little drama with some nig-gas. I guess nobody was feeling that I was back in Carol City but fuck it. This was my hood. I was here to stay and being that I was no stranger to letting muthafuckas know where I stood, I had to keep my glock on me at all times now. Miami was my hometown regardless of how long I was gone for. I moved how I wanted to move. Fuck what anybody thought.

I couldn't continue to fuck around with Kida for a few reasons, but the number one reason was because she was a leech. I knew from jump what type of female she was but being that we messed around in the past, I gave her the benefit of the doubt and tried to start fresh. Wrong fucking move. She only wanted my money and my dick. I mean, once I stacked my paper the way I really wanted to, I planned on settling down with a nice lil' shorty so we could raise some bad ass kids together. Unfortunately, I just didn't picture that type of lifestyle with Kida at all. I cut her ass off unknowingly, and she'd been blowing my phone up for the last two weeks with her bipolar rants. I was done with that.

I moved into a two-story townhouse and bought myself a 2020 Lincoln Navigator; all black with the custom chrome interior. My walk-in closet was to capacity and a nigga ate good every day and night, all thanks to the many soul food restaurants in my area. Heem, Saige, Teddy and I were all building a bond as a team. We kept shit on a need to know basis and strictly business and that was cool with me. Needless to say, I was living it up and the only piece to the puzzle I was missing was that special lady.

Pulling my truck out of the complex I lived in, I headed out for some breakfast. I was hung the fuck over from turning up at The Trill with Teddy last night and a nigga was starving per usual. I spent hella bread on take out. See, this is exactly why I need a bitch around the crib on some real shit.

*BOOM!*

"Fuck!" I cursed aloud. I'd just slammed into the back of a nice ass cranberry Range Rover. I turned my music down and got prepared to hop out. Shorty beat me to the punch.

"Oh, hell nah!" She exclaimed as she bent down to examine the damage in the back. "My fucking truck!" One of her taillights was hanging along with her license plate. Nothing too serious.

"My fault, sweetheart." I offered an apology. "I wasn't even…"

"Paying attention? Clearly!" She cut her eyes at me and stood to eyeball me up and down. With her arms folded across her chest, she said, "Uh huh, you probably don't even have a driver's license. You look like the type to hot box it." She nodded at my truck. "I bet that Nav's stolen, huh?" She scoffed and sucked her teeth then looked away. It was obvious she was pissed the fuck off.

I started to cuss her ignorant ass the fuck out until I realized who she was. The way she held her pouty lips and raised her perfectly arched eyebrows made me think back to the day she crossed in front of my car a couple months ago. We were in the same intersection now. How crazy was that? I was star struck. She was dressed to impress today; her pixie cut was now a deep red and she'd gained a few pounds but goddamn, she was gorgeous.

"Stolen?" I smirked at her then backed up to my whip. Reaching inside to the glove compartment, I pulled out my papers to show her this truck was in my name, so she had me sadly mistaken. "Excuse me, rudeness. A nigga is legit out this bitch." I flashed little miss attitude my papers and watched as her scowl turned into a slight frown. I laughed. "Damn, lighten up. I'll pay for ya whip to get fixed. It's nothing."

"Sounds good." She rolled her eyes and held her hand out.

Again, I laughed and took her hand in mine instead. Pulling her into me, I held her by the waist and replied, "How about you join me for breakfast instead?" I licked my lips at her little sexy ass. She stared up at me with a twinkle in her deep brown eyes. I was a big nigga and there was something about petite women that turned me the hell out. Suddenly, shorty broke our gaze and pulled away from me.

"Eww, I don't even know you like that!" She held up her hand to my face so I could see that she rocked a fat ass diamond ring. "I got a man so keep your chump change and petty date." Turning me all the way down and walking away, I couldn't help but watch her hips sway.

"Aye," I called out to her, intending to piss her off with my next line. She glanced my way as she swung her door open. I threw my hands up and asked, "What yo' man gotta do with me?" A wide grin appeared on my face.

"Ugh, boy please She dismissed me quicker than a bullied teacher on a Friday afternoon. Her Range screeched off.

Rubbing my hands together, I quickly jumped back in my truck. It was time to do some investigating now. I had let her ass walk away from me twice but I promised there wouldn't be a third time. I was determined to get the drop on shorty and set something up to get her in my presence again.

# PEYTON

I banged on Milah's front door like I was the muthafucking police. That's how mad a bitch was. Ever since my miscarriage two months ago, I become mad at the world, and I simply didn't give two fucks. Plus, my daddy was long gone. I was feeling so fucked up inside; I couldn't hide the pain. I was an open wound. My mother was taking my daddy's death hella hard, not to mention she held some sort of resentment against me for "ruining" her husband's funeral. Like, what the fuck? I couldn't control what happened that day! However, I could control the way I handled shit going forward. I needed to start looking out for P's best interest from here on out.

My relationship with Faheem took a turn for the worse the day I discovered I miscarried our first child. All I did was cry and lash out at him every single minute of the day. I was a wreck. But of course, after meeting with a therapist and best doctors recommended, they convinced me that it was very much possible for me to conceive again. My blood type was rare so there would be precautionary steps taken to ensure my child would be healthy the next go around. They weren't quite sure what went wrong with my previous pregnancy, but I was trying not to dwell on it as much. Faheem took all the blame for me losing the baby and went above and beyond to win me over again. I don't know what it is, but I could never stay mad at his ass for too long. I just didn't have it in me. I loved me some Heem no matter what.

Milah's front door cracked open and she peeked her big head out. Chuckling as she pulled her robe closed, she said, "What the...oh, hey best friend. W-W-What you doing here?"

"Girl," I started to say as I snatched my shades off. "I just had a run in a few blocks away. The back of my truck is all fucked up. Ugh, I need a damn drink!" I vented and tried to push my way inside but she stopped me.

"Alright, just gimmie a minute, kay?" She shut the door so fast, I couldn't even protest.

"Oh, no she didn't..." I gasped and leaned up against the door to see if I could hear voices. "Uh uh, Milah Ballard! Who you got up in there?" I banged on the door a few times. "You better open up this damn door, heffa!" Sure enough, I heard a very familiar voice on the other side of the door.

"Just open up the door."

My mouth fell open and my jaw dropped when Milah opened the door and this time all the way, so I could see inside. Standing in the doorway biting her nails, she looked back and forth between me and Teddy. I stepped inside eyeing them both.

"Ooooh," I said in a childlike voice, ready to snitch like a bitch. "Y'all up in here doing the nasty?"

"Shut up, Peyton!" Milah whined and swatted at me.

Teddy tossed on his white tee and grabbed his keys off the leather couch. "Now she knows, right?" He walked over to kiss Milah's lips, kissed my cheek and then shrugged his shoulders. "Y'all be easy." He slapped Milah's ass and just like that, he left my best friend's house.

She slammed the door behind him, flew past me and up the stairs into the bathroom. Of course, my ass was right on her heels, waiting for the fucking tea! This bitch tried to skip the conversation and jump right in the shower.

"Oh, hell nah, bitch," I grabbed Milah by the elbow before she started to take her clothes off. "Lucy, you got some 'splaining to do..." I folded my arms across my chest with a smirk on my face.

Milah covered her face and spoke in her hands when she said, "Ugh, why Peyton? Damn, what you want me to say?"

"Um, bitch, everything? You always said you'd never fuck with nobody in Faheem's crew because..." I imitated her annoying ass voice. "All them muthafuckas is just like Faheem...ain't shit!" I laughed.

Over these last eight years, Milah had a front row seat to all of my drama. She tolerated my relationship off the strength of me but deep down, it was no secret that she couldn't stand Faheem's ass. With Teddy living the exact same trap lifestyle, my best friend swore up and down that she just could not and would not get with the shits. Now I find them basically in the act of doing the nasty. I mean, Milah was grown and free to do as she damn well pleased. All I wanted to know was why she had a sudden change of heart and felt the need to hide the shit. She was crazy if she thought I was going to let this it go.

"So what's up?"

Sitting on the edge of the tub, Milah let out a deep ass sigh and looked up at me. She replied, "I don't know, P. There's just something about him that I fuck with. For starters, I haven't heard his name in the mouths of bitches in these streets, he doesn't have any kids, his money is hella long and his dick is even longer. Mmmm mmm mmm!" She closed her eyes as she reflected on their sex, I assumed. Truth be told, I didn't want to hear about that part. I held my hand up to stop her from continuing with that part of the conversation.

"Eww, bitch. Please stop. I do not wanna

know that shit." I rubbed my ears before continuing. "So, is that your *nigga nigga*, or just some dick for the season?" I squinted my eyes and pointed a finger at her ass. "I know you, Millz. You never stay with a nigga long enough to know his real name." She flashed me her middle finger.

"Well, we all know Teddy's name is Theodore, bitch." I twisted my face up at her sarcasm while she grinned up at me. "I swear, this time it's different, best friend." I simply shook my head and Milah continued, "Look, P, we been fucking around for a couple months now and it's been crazy as hell tryna keep this shit from you."

"Why were you keeping it from me anyway?"

"'Cause I didn't want hear the "do better" speech, nor did I wanna see the look that you got on your face right now." It was then I realized I was mean mugging the shit out of her, and I relaxed my facial muscles.

I sighed and replied, "Milah, you're a grown ass woman. You know right from wrong and if you feel like Teddy is the right choice, then who the hell am I to stop you? Just don't be hiding shit from me. That's shady, best friend."

She nodded her head and stood up to hug me. "You got that. I'm sorry."

"Apology accepted." She took her nightie

off and jumped in the shower as I sat on the toilet seat. "Now can I tell you about the nigga who slammed into my car a lil' while ago?"

She peeked her head out the shower and asked, "Was he cute? Did he look like he had some money?"

I dropped my head in laughter. "Here you go! Will you focus on the situation? Dang!"

She laughed as well and replied, "My bad. Go 'head."

I went on to describe the run in with ol' boy and then told Milah he asked me out on a date. "I swear, the audacity of these niggas. Girl, that shit had me hot for real." I fumed. "Then he had the nerve to ask me what my man had to do with him. Tuh, ol' slimin' ass nigga." I shuddered. Milah hopped out the shower, wrapped herself up in a towel then faced me with a smirk. "What?" I asked, innocently.

"I know you just as well as you know my ass, and I can hear the curiosity dripping from your voice." She moved closer to me with squinted eyes, pointing her long ass finger at me. "You secretly wish you'd asked for his name and number, huh?"

"Say what?" I sucked my teeth and waved her off. "Man, please. You tripping, Millz." I rubbed the back of my neck and looked away from her gaze. "I got a man…"

She stepped closer to the sink to brush her pearly whites. "Well, what ya man gotta do with me?" She snickered. "Look, the nigga hit your car, best friend. There's no harm in finding him to see what's good with a repayment for damages." Milah winked at me through the mirror.

I balanced my weight from left to right, contemplating my next move. I guess she was kind of right. I could get the damages fixed on my truck then cruise around looking for that distinct Navigator. I slightly smiled at the idea because it sounded crazy as hell to go looking for a nigga I knew nothing about. I mean, he was finer than wine with a witty sense of humor. Plus, he did already offer to pay for the damages up front. No harm, no foul in taking him up on his offer.

I gave in. "Alright, but your ass riding with me on this and no pillow talking either, bitch."

# MILAH

*"So, is it true? You been wanting to see what this mouth do?" I asked as I gripped his dick through his jeans and my pussy got excited. I was drunk as shit and feeling bold as fuck. Teddy had his back against the wall and he licked his lips as we stared each other down.*

*"So, what's good with it?" He asked and I hurriedly locked the door of the men's bathroom. Then, a bitch dropped to her knees and went crazy on his dick.*

*We were in Seaspice Restaurant celebrating Peyton's birthday with Faheem and the crew. I don't know if it was all the shots that made us hornier or what but the vibe could be felt all night. Now usually, I ignore Teddy's flirting and shit but tonight, I entertained his ass. As soon as I saw him stumble away to use the bathroom, I followed inside. Let's be honest, what nigga turns down head? Especially not from a head slayer like myself. I deep throated his dick until he hit my tonsils then spit on it and slurped it up. Glancing up at him, I peeped he had his eyes closed and I knew I had him.*

*I toyed with my pussy while I sucked him off. With a combination of deep throating, wrist action and this heavenly tongue on his balls, I had Teddy cumming in six minutes flat. That was actually a new record for me, but when I was hella into the dick I was sucking, shit... it was a wrap. My goal was to taste his cum and swallow every drop. Done deal. Without hesitation, he bent me over the bathroom sink and whipped out a condom.*

*I looked back at him and asked, "Why can't I feel you without that shit?" I stroked his dick. He looked at me like I had eight heads.*

*"'Cause I don't know who else you out here giving this lil' pussy to. I wanna fuck but a nigga ain't stupid, shawty. Now bend over and take this dick," He slipped on a magnum and worked his way inside, groaning loudly. "Damn, yo' shit tight as fuck." After he was just talking all that shit, I just simply smiled and threw this ass back.*

*I was on my bullshit at the time and not really fucking with these niggas in Miami. Most nights, it was my two fingers and Porn Hub so I wasn't surprised my pussy was tight. I clapped my ass as I backed it up on him and my pussy started getting happy. Teddy was rubbing all over my ass. I taunted him, "Uh huh, what was all that bullshit you was saying? You know this pussy fire." We fucked hard body for like a good ten minutes before I felt the convulsions hit me.*

*"Goddamn, yo' pussy going crazy. Shit, Milah." I grabbed hold of the edge of the sink and closed my eyes as he hit my pussy harder and harder. "I'm bouta cum with you." Holding me firmly by my shoulders,*

*this nigga kept fucking the shit out of me until his nut was emptied into the condom. "Damn, that was a good lil' quickie. Lemme find out, Millz." Teddy slapped my assed and grabbed some paper towels to clean off.*

*Wiping between my legs, I smiled at him and replied, "Nigga, now you know. Stop being stingy with the dick. I know how to keep a secret."*

That was six months ago. As I wiped the corners of my mouth, I listened to Teddy's ass complain about Peyton finding out about us fucking around. I sat in the passenger seat of his black Lambo thinking the conversation was done. Since earlier, he was on some bullshit and I was just trying to end the night on a better note. I figured sucking his dick would work but nope, he kept going on and on.

"I don't like muthafuckas knowing my business. If you haven't figured out by now, I'mma real low-key ass nigga, Milah. If you gon' be out here broadcasting what we do and shit, we can stop right the fuck now." He lashed out at me as we sat in front of my crib. Zipping his jeans, he glared over at me. I wanted to cuss him out for his fucking attitude but I knew better. Teddy was sexy as hell but shorter than I usually liked my niggas. Right now, his cocky, short ass had me twisted.

At twenty-seven, my money wasn't long and I didn't have it that great. Unlike Peyton, I watched my mama struggle with men in the home all my life and she could never keep a job. I should have known to do better but I was just following in her footsteps. It's been years since I'd held a position at some job but going back to school for some shit did cross my mind here and there. For now, I was basically living off of what a nigga would give me and what I chose to settle for. Cool by me. It'd been working for years now. I just didn't know why I couldn't hold onto a nigga. I was pretty as shit; brown skin, slim thick, tall and I could dress my ass off. But for some reason, niggas just didn't see forever in me regardless of what I'd do for them or how hard I was trying to fuck with them.

So, now I was looking for love. I was looking for a come up and Teddy was it. Whatever attitude he kicked down to me had to be deaded but I wasn't losing out this time around. I was tired of fucking just to get a bill or two paid or have some pocket change to do a lil' something. I knew there was no way I would fuck with Faheem so I figured the only way I would be content and get a glimpse of the good life was to fuck with someone in his crew. He told me to keep shit between me and him and I planned on keeping it that way. Peyton's ass popping up at my crib was not part of the plan and she damn near ruined everything. Although Teddy made it seem like he was cool with her finding out in front of the both of us, he made it very clear to me that evening shit wasn't cool at all.

89

"Broadcasting?" Getting back to the conversation, I looked at this nigga like he was stupid. "But weren't you the one who told me to open the door? You could have hidden somewhere, ya know..." I reminded him with a roll of the eyes.

"You getting smart with me?" He glanced in my direction. I sighed and reluctantly shook my head no. He continued, "Look, P's like family. Now that I think about it, she ain't one of these loud-mouth bitches." He pondered, rubbing his sexy ass beard.

"So, what's the problem, boo?" I snuggled up close to him and kissed his cheek. "We good, right?" I bit my lip and turned his face towards mine. Shit, I was hoping we were. He was kicking me down some dough as long as I let him stash drugs in my crib. My rent, bills and my car note were paid, plus I always had good money now to do whatever I wanted. I wasn't going anywhere, and I was going to make sure I kept my claws in Teddy for as long as possible.

# FAHEEM

"Sayona, what I gotta do to get you to get this abortion? Huh? Name yo' fucking price!"

It was a brisk morning and a nigga was up before the birds. I had to do everything in my power to convince this bitch Sayona not to go through with this pregnancy. She was approaching the danger zone for getting an abortion. I didn't need that kind of negativity in my life right now, especially with Peyton recently losing our baby. I'd never hear the end of this shit. She'd try to kill my ass and easily take that insanity plea.

Sayona was a lil' freak bitch I'd met one late night at the gas station a while back. She was a pretty chick with a pretty mouth and an aggressive yet cool ass personality. I wanted to hit it plus, she liked to sniff white here and there so I figured I could kill two birds. We started fucking around and sure enough, her ass popped up pregnant...with twins! Then she had the nerve to steal Peyton's number out of my phone one night when I was drunk as fuck and started calling her up, telling her about the shit. Sayona told her how I was ignoring her because she was pregnant. It was true but still, this bitch violated in a major way and I had to put an end to this shit now.

"You think you can make babies then pull this sucka shit, Heem? I didn't beg you to nut in me all them fucking times." Sayona slid off the hood of her car and approached me all brawlic. "You knew what you were doing just as I did. I can't believe you right now! You ol' disrespectful ass muthafucka!" She shoved me in the chest.

I dropped my head in my hands as I responded, "Sayona, I cannot do this with you, my nigga. I can't." Tears streamed down her face as she balled up her fists and scowled at me.

"They're fucking twins, Faheem! Twins!" Sayona moved close to me and wrapped her arms around my neck trying to lay her head on my chest. I pushed her off of me. She pleaded with me. "Please. Why you doing me like this?"

This bitch was getting me hot! She wasn't cooperating, and I'd had enough of this bullshit. I could not have any more babies on Peyton, especially not now. I wasn't risking what I had with her for nobody. These bitches had me fucked up. I snatched Sayona up by her throat and watched as her eyes bulged out of her head. She clawed at my wrists. I didn't give a fuck that we were in public for muthafuckas to see either.

"Aye, let me be clear!" I barked. "You were just a convenient fuck on some late nights and that's it! Why the fuck you wanna have my kids, cuh? Huh? Why? You looking for a come up, and I been told you what type of time I'm on, my nigga. I ain't that nigga." I reminded her and pushed her down on the ground. Hovering over her whimpering ass, I continued, "Now do I have to stomp those muthafuckas outta you or what?"

Sayona stared up at me in disbelief with hurt written all over her face. She held her protruding belly and asked, "Are you really serious right now, Heem? Like...for real? I've never been pregnant before. You want me to just up and kill my babies for you?"

"Either you can, or I will. Plain and fucking simple." I stood over her and eyeballed the shit out of her. "So, what the fuck will it be? I ain't got all fucking morning to be playing around with yo' ass." I checked the time on my watch.

She struggled to get back on her feet. Winded, she replied, "Fine, fine. I'll do it." She wiped her tears and sniffled. "But I'mma need..." Without hesitation, I pulled out a knot of money, peeled off two hundred dollar bills and tossed them at her simple ass.

"I'll schedule yo' appointment and bring you so be on the lookout for my call in a few days." I walked back over to where my car was parked then looked back as she began to walk down the street. "Aye!" I called out to her. She turned around with a smile. I continued, "Don't try no disappearing shit either, or I'll make ya ass disappear for good, understand?" I watched as Sayona sadly shook her head and carried her ass along. I told myself that's what I get for fucking around with a baby. She was only nineteen and still learning a lot in life. She had a rude awakening fucking with a nigga like me.

\*\*\*

After that little run in, I made my rounds to check up on my corner boys grab some dough and chop it up with some niggas. Peyton was on my mind heavy this morning. I knew she was probably going to be pissed that I wasn't home when she woke up, but I always had business to tend to. She knew that. Shit had been going smoothly for us lately.

I stopped by this flower shop to grab my baby some roses then headed to her store, Youth Lot. I wanted to surprise her to show her a nigga was really out here trying to be a better nigga. Just then, my phone rang. It was Syncere calling probably to link up. I answered, "What it do, cuh? You good?"

He replied, "Man, I'm always good, big dawg." I laughed because this nigga stayed calling me that like we weren't just a few years apart. He continued, "I wanted to holla you about that nigga Marco. Cuh, that lil' nigga wilding out here running his mouth about that shit last weekend. Next thing you know, we gon' be burying his ass."

I shook my head and rubbed my beard. Marco was eighteen years old and a hot head type of nigga. One wrong word and he'd be quick to bust his gun no matter who you were. He bodied one of the lil' niggas he got murder smoke with last weekend. I cleared shit up and told the nigga to lay low for a while. Clearly, this boy was tired of being cooped up in his mother's basement, but that didn't mean brag about the shit around town. The nigga he shot didn't even die; he was fucked up in a wheelchair for the rest of his life. But, karma always came back around, especially if you didn't kill the person. This was just another problem on my hands. Shit was getting crazy with them young boys. I'd hate to be the one making funeral arrangements for anybody on my team.

"Good looking out on the info, cuh." I told Syncere. "I'll speak to him about that shit. Don't even trip on it."

"I know you gon' handle that, big dawg. I was just letting you know. Also, I got that for you whenever you ready for it so we can keep this shit going."

I smirked. "That's what a nigga likes to hear, cuh. You wild with it, boy." I pulled up in front of Peyton's store.

"True, true."

"What else you got going on?" I cut the engine and sat back.

"Ain't shit. I think I done ran into my future baby mama the other day, so I'mma try to get with her ass." He laughed.

I laughed back and nodded my head. "Oh yeah? That's what's up. As long as she ain't ratchet like Kida's ass then she Gucci in my book, cuh."

"Oh, nah. Shorty's legit. I can tell off the rip."

"I feel that. Good shit. I'm actually about to go check my bitch right now. I'mma get with you." I scooped up the roses and exited my truck.

"Aight. One hunnid."

I ended the call as I stepped foot inside Youth Lot. Taking my shades off, I looked around feeling proud. I admired the spot and had to give Peyton credit. Business was booming, and the customers seemed genuinely happy. My bitch was a success and I respected her grind. Of course, I spoiled her with whatever she wanted, but I loved that she had her own hustle. That shit was sexy as fuck to me. I needed to start appreciating her ass for real. I couldn't help but smile at the thought of her, but that smile quickly faded when I heard an annoying sound.

"Well, well, well," Diamond, the sales associate, approached me pushing a rack of clothes. "Look what the garbage men done dropped off."

She rolled her hazel eyes at me. She sported the ill stank face.

I ignored her smart remark about me. See, me and Diamond had a brief lil' thing going on about a year ago when she first moved to Miami. She approached my brother and I as we were leaving the strip club one night and asked if she could go home with us. Diamond was a bad chocolate thing with a cute face and fast ass and her eyes made her stand out. She was making money out the strip club selling Molly, but she didn't want to live that lifestyle anymore because niggas was always trying fuck. She told me I seemed like the type to have a better opportunity for her but she knew she would have to prove herself. I damn sure wasn't putting her onto a kilo but at the time, Peyton was feeling overwhelmed with Youth Lot as it got busier and I figured she could use some help. So, and I smashed Diamond and to be honest, her lil' twenty-one-year-old pussy was aight. I couldn't even front. Afterwards, I had her resume hooked up and Peyton was so impressed with her that she hired her on the spot. They hit it off right away and I kept hitting Diamond off whenever I wanted to, up until the bitch wanted to get greedy and start asking for money. She even threatened to tell my bitch everything, including the baby she aborted along the way. Every two weeks like fucking payroll, I had to broke Diamond off with some dough to keep her mouth shut. Shit was becoming annoying and the only reason I kept her alive was because I didn't really want to kill the bitch and have that bloodshed on my hands. It wasn't worth it. But the smart remakes and side eyes were getting on my fucking nerves. Shit had to stop eventually one way or another.

"Where P at?" I looked Diamond up and down thinking to myself, *why she gotta be so annoying and crazy? She's too cute. Damn...*

She smirked and popped her lips at me then said, "She's in the back on a business call. You gon' have my money on Friday, right?" She placed her hands on her hips.

I eyeballed this bitch with disgust and responded, "Girl, watch out." I brushed past her, heading for the back office.

"You know what time it is, Faheem..." Diamond said loudly behind me. I turned briefly to look back at her evil ass. She winked and smirked devilishly.

*I should body this bitch right now*, I thought as I knocked on Peyton's office door and entered at the same time. She smiled and put her finger up for me to be silent while she finished her call. I laid the roses on the desk and walked around to where she was seated.

"Of course, Mr. Lee. I can assist you with that." She swatted me away as I proceeded to unbutton her peach colored blouse. I kissed her neck and watched her shudder. She cleared her throat and tried to continue with the conversation, "Um, yes, I'm here. Next Saturday? S-S-Sure..." I cupped her titties and sucked on her neck while trying to hide my laughter. Peyton squirmed at my touch and her breathing changed. "Oh...um, okay Mr. Lee. That's great. Just come by the store then. Have a great day." She rushed off the phone, stood up abruptly and we tongued each other down. After a few moments, we came up for air. She walked over to lock the door then said, "I can't believe you. Got me sounding all stupid on the phone and shit."

Laughing, I said, "Sorry, baby. I couldn't help myself. You looking good as fuck. Goddamn!"

She fingered the roses on the desk with a wide smile then picked them up to smell them. "These are beautiful. Are they mine?"

"Of course. Who else would I be buying roses for?"

Peyton strutted her sexy ass over to me, looking all seductive and shit. Suddenly, her sexy gaze turned murderous. I watched as her eyes got squinty as fuck and her nostrils flared. "Muthafucka!" She hauled off and punched the shit out of me.

"Yo', what the fuck?!" I instantly got hot.

My eyebrows bunched together in bewilderment. "The fuck was that for?"

She aggressively grabbed at my Polo collar and replied, "Nigga, what bitch was you all hugged up with wearing purple lipstick?" She questioned angrily.

"What?" My ass tried looking down at my collar as if I didn't know I was already caught up. Fucking Sayona being all dramatic and shit earlier! I closed my eyes. Peyton shoved me in the chest.

"You better be praying to God, my nigga. You wanna play dumb like you don't know the bitch you was just with? I can't believe I fell for this 'good guy' act you been putting on these last few weeks." She punched me in the chest and I bit my bottom lip. She was getting me hot. "You still fucking around on me, Heem? Still?!" She shouted then slapped the shit out of me. This time that bitch stung a little bit. I grabbed her wrists and pinned her little ass against the wall.

"P, stop putting yo' fucking hands on me!" I yelled in her face. "The fuck? You crazy? I wasn't doing shit! If you'd let me explain..."

She struggled to get away from me. "Nigga, fuck ya explanation!" Tears welled up in her eyes. "Why you keep doing this shit to me? You don't fucking love me, nigga. It's impossible! You weren't even home this morning so lemme guess, you was at another early morning meeting?" She spit the biggest, nastiest spit ball right in my eyes. "I hate you!" That's when a nigga snapped and I slapped her ass up twice real quick. Peyton fell to the floor crying.

"Oh shit…" *Did I really just do that shit? What the fuck…?* I was tripping hard. I'd never put my hands on Peyton ever. She was my queen. I didn't know what came over me in that moment. I lost it when she got disrespectful.

She held her cheek with a shocked look on her face. Her left eye bubbled up quickly. She cried, "Oh, my God! Did you just fucking hit me? Have you lost ya fuckin' mind?"

"Baby," I reached out for her. "I keep telling you to stop putting yo' hands on me. I'm sorry though." I bent down to help her up and she scooted far away from me.

She screamed. "Leave me the fuck alone, Faheem!" With a tear stained face, she cried, "Get the fuck out! Go!" I rubbed my hands over my face as this uneasy feeling settled in my stomach. I'd just hit my future wife. I shook my head as I stood up to leave.

"P, I'm sorry…"

"Get the fuck out, Faheem! NOW!" She curled up on the floor crying hysterically.

"I love you." I hesitated on leaving and then hurriedly got the fuck up out of the store before somebody called the police on a nigga.

# CHAPTER FIVE

# PEYTON

*"I've been to hell and now I'm back again and every now and then love don't love me..."* I cried and sang along to Kim Davis as she poured out her heart and soul on the track. She was literally singing my life and the shit hurt so badly. *"But I can't convince you. I can't make you believe. I won't convince you that I'm all the girl you need..."*

The tears clouded my vision as I drove along the lonely highway. I'd been driving around for hours bumping R&B songs in my feelings. I couldn't figure out where we went wrong or better yet, where I went wrong. All I ever did was be the best bitch I could ever be and where did that leave me? Smacked up and heartbroken over and over again. It was a never-ending story and I wanted it to end. It wasn't supposed to be like this. My daddy was gone, my mama still wasn't speaking to me, I lost my first child, my sister was MIA and my nigga was tearing me the fuck down slowly but surely. I felt broken inside. I didn't want to hurt anymore.

I pulled my car over on the side of the road, left the keys in the ignition with the engine running, then proceeded to walk along the bridge to the Miami River. This was it. I cried, "Daddy, I miss you so much. I just wanna be with you. You'll make everything feel better. You'll make it right again." I placed a hand over my fast beating heart. "I love you." Closing my eyes, I said a quick prayer as hot tears streamed down my face. This was the end. The time was now. "I love you..." I took a deep breath.

"You don't wanna do that."

My eyes flew open, and I looked up at the dark sky in amazement. "Daddy?" I questioned then somebody scooped me up from the edge of the bridge and planted me on my feet. It was *him*.

He said, "We could work towards all that daddy shit, sweetheart."

It was Mr. Cool that hit the back of my Rover the other day. Butterflies invaded my belly as a wave of embarrassment took over me. I felt foolish for my actions, and I knew I probably looked crazy. Stupid crazy. Crazy stupid. I wiped my tears.

He gave me a concerned look and lifted my face up towards his. He licked his lips and gazed deep into my eyes. I swallowed hard as he cupped my face and we stared each other down. Neither of us said a word for a few moments. However, he was the one to speak first.

"Please tell me you weren't about to jump, sweetheart."

I sniffled and shifted uncomfortably. Glancing down at my feet, I nodded my head 'yes'. My words were stuck in my throat for some odd reason. I felt a little lightheaded as well.

"I'm Syncere, take this walk with me." He gently took my hand into his and I skeptically looked up at him, giving him the side eye. He said, "I won't hurt you. Just come sit with me for a minute. Please."

A car drove by us as we walked over to his Navigator. He opened the passenger side door and lifted me up by my hips. Syncere hopped in the driver's seat and glanced over at my running car just sitting there then he looked at me.

"I know you don't know me from a fucking hole in the wall but I keep crossing paths with you. I mean, it's gotta be for a reason. Shit, maybe it was for this reason right now."

I sighed and laid my head against the headrest. "I told you. I got a man."

"Sweetheart, with all due respect, if you had a man, he would never let you be out this late by yo'self about to end yo' precious life." He stated matter-of-factly then lifted my hand and asked me, "What's yo' name, beautiful?"

I started to give my full name and then opted not to. Shit, Faheem knew too many people in this wild ass city. It would be just my luck. So instead, I said, "Call me P."

He smiled at me and I chuckled softly, allowing my shoulders to drop a little bit. Something in his tone of voice and his vibe made me feel safe and instantly comfortable. It was definitely a little weird. I looked at my watch then looked at the bridge and finally at my car. I let out a huge sigh and replied, "I think I should go."

It was after midnight and my phone had been dead for hours. I knew Milah was tripping and Faheem had probably sent a search team out for my ass. I quickly made the decision to sleep at Milah's crib for the night. I prayed like hell she was home with her night owl ass. Syncere held my hand firmly in his then with his free hand, he reached over and turned my face towards his once more.

Looking deep into my eyes, he asked, "You gon' be alright? I'd appreciate if you'd let me follow you to yo' destination." I raised an eyebrow and he laughed at me. "A nigga ain't crazy or no shit like that. I just wanna know you safe and sound. That's all." He crossed his heart.

I squinted my eyes at him and for some strange reason or another, I believed him. I allowed him to follow me to Milah's spot. I plugged my phone up to charge along the way. About thirty minutes later, I pulled up a few houses down from her crib with Syncere right behind me. Hopping out of my truck with my phone and purse, I approached his truck. He rolled down his window and flashed me a pearly white smile. I chuckled and told him, "Thank you."

"For what exactly, sweetheart?"

"Everything." I gazed at him. "Seriously. I was having a bad mental break and it was like God sent you at the right time. I'm beyond grateful. Thank you."

Syncere shrugged and said, "Just call me yo' guardian angel then." He winked at me and gripped the steering wheel. "I'm saying though, I guess you owe me yo' or something like that."

I laughed. "I should have seen that shit coming." I toyed around with the idea then said, "Nah, but um...you can definitely give me yours. How's that?"

His sexy ass rubbed his beard and nodded his head. He replied, "A woman who compromises. I love it." He rattled off his number then started his truck back up. "I look forward to hearing from you, Pretty P. Be easy."

I stepped onto the sidewalk and waved as he drove off. I stared at the number I'd just entered into my phone then checked my notifications. I had thirty-seven text messages and missed calls from Faheem but, at that moment, none of that shit mattered to me. I saved Syncere's number then blocked Faheem and took my ass down the street.

# SYNCERE

I lay in bed that night staring up at the ceiling, smoking a fat ass blunt and thinking about P. I couldn't believe I saved ol' girl from jumping to her death. That shit was deep as fuck and it had me wondering why she was even going to do that shit in the first place. Like, what could she be going through to have her in that weak state of mind? I mean, you shouldn't judge a book by its cover, but judging her from her looks, she seemed to have it good. Whoever her nigga was, he was clearly slipping and missing all the signs. I vibed out to Travis Scott and fell asleep with her weighing heavy on my mind.

When I woke up later that afternoon, I noticed I didn't have a single missed call or text from her ass. I laughed it off and hoped she was alright. She had my mind occupied. I already dreamed of our wedding day and shit, and I barely knew anything about her. I had to see her ass again but for now, I hopped out of the bed and got ready to start my day. Faheem called a meeting for this evening and I already knew it was about this street shit. I'd never had street drama until now trying to keep shit cool with these young boys out here and I'd be damned if I spent eight years locked up like an animal just to go out in a box behind niggas getting money. What type of shit was these niggas on?

I showered, got dressed and decided to go check on this nigga Teddy. Lately, he'd been wilding with the coke, pulling disappearing acts and his money was starting to come up short. The first time it happened, it appeared to be a mistake and Teddy came back to Faheem with the right amount. However, the second time, I noticed shit wasn't adding up and put up three bands to make up the difference. Faheem didn't seem to peep the fuck up. I mean, damn, I knew the product niggas was moving was some grease but still, that didn't mean Teddy's ass had to get sloppy to support his fucking habit. Granted Faheem knew my cousin longer than me, he was starting to place more responsibility on me, and I could see this shit ending badly if he ever caught on to what Teddy was doing. There could not be a third fuck up for this nigga, and I was going to see to that shit.

I smoked about two blunts to the face and bombed on some Cinnamon Toast Crunch before getting myself together. My thoughts circled back around to P' sexy ass. Damn. We both got our whips fixed but I still needed a way to get back in her presence regardless if she had a nigga or not. Shit, she looked like she could cook too. I needed all that.

Just as I hopped in my Nav to head to

Teddy's neck of the woods, my phone rang and I peeped it was him calling. I answered, "Yo, cuh. I was just about to come check ya ass."

A female cried into the phone, "He's been shot! They shot him! There was so much fucking blood!"

I looked at the phone thinking this nigga was playing games and said, "Yo, who the fuck is this?"

"What? Syncere, Nina! I was just getting ready to bring the twins outside when somebody drove by and started spraying." Teddy's baby's mother explained. "I'm surprised I'm not hit, he's all fucked up!" She cried hysterically into the phone.

"What the fuck? Where you at? Where's this nigga?" I questioned.

Nina sobbed, "He told me to call you right before they closed the doors on me."

"Mercy?" I busted an illegal U-Turn and headed that same way. "Man, that shit is far from this nigga's crib."

"Syncere, I don't know what to do! He had a gun on him and some work. I took everything and brought the shit in the crib." She explained with a shaky voice. "Oh, my God! What if the twins never see they daddy again?!"

"Listen! Calm down, please." I snapped at her. I couldn't take all that fucking screaming in my ear. "Nina, where you at?" I asked her again.

Sniffling, she answered, "I stay over in the apartments, Cypress Grove."

"Aight, sit tight and if the cops come around asking questions, don't say shit." Ending the call, I called up Faheem as I sped down the street. I told him to postpone that meeting because if my cousin died, there was sure to be a lot of dead muthafuckas in Miami.

# FAHEEM

"Damn boo, you good?"

I glanced over at Lala sitting in my passenger seat, ready to finish sucking me off but my mind was elsewhere at that moment. I was hotter than a bitch that shit didn't go as I planned. Teddy's ass was supposed to be dead, zipped up in a body bag, not on the way to the hospital with a chance of survival. See, I'd found out this nigga was stealing product from me to support his habit. I didn't give a fuck that he was sniffing the shit. He was grown and he could do as he pleased but fucking with my money was a fucking issue. He of all people knew what happened to muthafuckas who tried to get over on me.

I let the shit slide the first time but the second time, it was very clear that some fuck shit was going on. So, I paid some young niggas to follow this nigga Teddy for a couple of days and to catch that nigga lacking. When the time was right, they were supposed to shoot that nigga dead. He must've had a guardian angel watching over him to have survived the hit because my young boys told me they merked that nigga. Whether I considered you my close friend or not, all bets were off once I found out some sneaky shit was going on. I didn't give a fuck and Teddy's ass was no exception.

"Hello?" Lala used her pointy ass nail to turn my face towards her. "You alright? Can I finish what I started or nah?" She smirked at me.

My dick went soft as soon as I got that call and now, she was tripping. I wasn't interested in busting a fucking nut. I had to do some serious damage control to make sure this nigga Teddy never found out I ordered a hit on him if he survived. I prayed like hell he didn't. I had to bounce. Zipping my jeans, I shook my head and dryly replied, "Nah."

She scoffed. "What?"

I pulled some money out of my pockets and tossed them on her lap before starting my whip back up. We were sitting in her parking lot, so she was lucky she didn't have to take a cab back home. She ought to feel lucky. "Look, I'mma get with you a lil' later, Lala. I gotta bust this move right quick."

Lala looked down at the money in her lap then back up at me with a look that could kill. She sucked her teeth, shook her head then shoved the hundreds in her bra before buttoning her yellow blouse back up. "You know what, this shit's getting old, Heem. Real fucking old. You treat me like I'm just some hoe sometimes and that shit ain't cool. How long we been doing this shit? Six plus

TASHA MARIE

years?" She cut her eyes at me and hopped out of my truck, slamming the passenger door.

"Aye, come on, Lala. You know-"

"What time it is." She finished my sentence and leaned down in the window with a scowl on her pretty face. "One of these fucking days you gon' realize how much of a real bitch I am to you and I could be *that* bitch for you. It ain't always gotta be about sex and money." She told me and then flipped me off. "But go 'head, my nigga. Handle yo' business and continue to shit on my feelings." She stepped back and folded her arms across her chest, staring me down. I shook my head with annoyance and pulled off on her ass.

My thoughts switched to Peyton and I called her phone for the umpteenth time. It went straight to voicemail and I couldn't tell whether her shit was just dead. or her ass had me blocked. Either way, she was pissing me the fuck off. She was acting like I'd beat her ass or something. Granted I didn't mean to slap her at all, this was something we could get passed if she allowed it. I texted Milah and told her to keep my bitch there as long as possible until I got there. Fuck that. The thought of P leaving had me sick!

When I got to Mercy Medical, the shit was a zoo. The waiting room was full but I spotted Syncere sitting in the back consoling Teddy's mother. I got myself in check and approached

116

them both.

"Damn, cuh. This shit crazier than a muthafucka." I dapped up Syncere and asked, "You good?"

"I'm holding," he responded then I focused my attention on Teddy's mother.

"How you doing, Ms. Jackie?" I bent down to hug her and surprisingly, she slapped the shit out of me. Needless to say, a nigga was shocked. "What the fuck?"

"Auntie, what's good?" Syncere looked surprised himself.

"You devil! This is all your fault" Jackie lashed out at me. Crying, she started to attack me in the waiting room. "You did this!!! You no good, drug dealing, low life, raggedy muthafucka! GET THE FUCK OUT!!!"

"Aye, chill the fuck out!" I spoke through clenched teeth. She was drawing unnecessary attention towards us and I had my glock tucked on me with some work in my whip. She was wilding right now. Her words had me questioning if she knew anything, but I quickly dismissed that thought and chalked it up to her speaking out of anger.

"My fault, cuh. She's just a mess right now." Syncere held her back. "Auntie, it's all good. Teddy gon' be aight. I promise you that."

I grilled the both of them and said, "I'm out, cuh, before they call muthafucking security on niggas. Ms. Jackie, I'm sor-"

"Fuck you!" She spat in my direction.

I wanted to slap this old bitch in her sagging ass face but instead I did the smart thing. I got the fuck up out of that hospital and sped off to link with them young boys. Fuck waiting to see if Teddy pulled through. I had to kill them lil' niggas before word got around.

# CHAPTER SIX

# PEYTON

Until last night, I'd never blocked Faheem before but to me, our relationship had reached the ultimate low. For him to put hands on me, his future wife, over these bitches was ridiculous. Nah, he was all the way wrong and I was gon' make that nigga feel that shit too.

"You know you can stay here as long as you need to, best friend," Milah said to me as she entered her bedroom holding a bottle of Remy and a glass full. I stretched, yawned and cracked my neck. I'd slept the whole day away and my whole body was tense. A drink was what I definitely needed. It may have only been four in the afternoon but shit, it was five o'clock somewhere. I took the drink from her as she continued, "Eventually you'll tell me what really happened last night and why you showed up at my doorstep looking a mess at one in the morning, but hey, you know…" she shrugged. "I won't press you." She stared me down and gave me a look that said otherwise.

I lied and told her I'd been out chilling with Faheem all night then, insisted that he drop me off at her crib because he got a business call. Milah didn't question shit right then and there. She just let me in, pissed off that I'd broken her sleep, and we knocked right out in her bed. I broke her gaze, took a sip of the Remy and contemplated telling her the full truth or not. I honestly didn't want anyone knowing Faheem had hit me or that I was ready to end my life last night. It was kind of embarrassing to say the least.

Milah plopped down next to me and hugged me close. She said, "Come on, girl. You know you can come to me with anything. You know this."

I sighed, downed my glass and put it on the coaster on the nightstand. Turning to face, I told her the partial truth. I mentioned yet another heated argument over some bitch and how I had gotten to that moment of weakness. I couldn't help it as the tears began to flow. "He's draining the life out of me, Millz." I cried into my hands. "Love ain't supposed to feel like a one-way street. I'm tired of feeling like I'm the only one who wants this relationship. I'm a good woman."

"So," she paused as if trying to process all of what I'd just admitted to her. "Lemme get this straight. You was just ready to jump to your death 'cause a nigga don't know how to appreciate you?" She gave me a weird look. I shook my head and scooted away from her.

"See, I knew you wouldn't understand. Just forget it."

"No, help me understand, P. I mean, you're better than that and I know *you* know that shit."

"I know, I know. I don't know what came over me." I sighed heavily. "Look, I love Faheem with all my heart and I know that nigga loves me. I just don't get why he keeps shitting on me." I sniffled and shrugged my shoulders. "It's like he's so concerned with other bitches that the nigga can't even see how unhappy I am. I mean, here I am scared to even give another nigga my damn number." I vented and let out a sad chuckle. I twirled my engagement ring then looked up at my best friend with tears in my eyes. "We've been together for eight years, Milah. Engaged for two. Why haven't we set a date or even had an engagement party?" I shook my head in disappointment.

Milah turned up the Remy bottle and took a huge gulp as her fingered tapped around her phone screen. She shook off the strong taste and then responded, "Listen, Peyton. Aside from the bullshit, you have it good. Shit, better than most bitches including me. Plus, you're a strong, independent woman with a boss ass nigga who would give you the world on a diamond studded platter if you asked for it."

"And that's the fucking problem," I interjected with my hand up. "I shouldn't have to ask for it. I deserve the world and then some and I keep trying to make him see that shit. What's a bitch to do, walk away or continue to be walked all over?" I asked her. "Come on, Millz, even you would be like 'enough is enough'." I chuckled.

"Hmmm, maybe so but I also don't own my own business nor do I have a nigga like Faheem." She rolled her eyes at me. I watched as she took another swig of the Remy and slammed the bottle down on her nightstand. Turning to face me, Milah said, "So you gotta share yo' nigga every once in a while. Big deal. Do I like Faheem's ass? Not particularly. Do I think you could find better?" She shrugged and flipped her long hair over her shoulder and added, "Probably not." Looking me dead in my eyes, she continued on with her opinions, "Best friend, I think you need to count your blessings, especially after last night. Suck the shit up and go on back home to yo' paid ass nigga."

She walked off and out of her bedroom, leaving me sitting there with my mouth hanging wide open. A bitch was indeed speechless! I'm talking floored! Milah ain't never took up for Faheem on a good day and here she was basically pushing me back into his arms. I sat there torn in between cussing her ass out, unblocking my nigga so we could figure this shit out. Nah, I could be alone and miserable then again, I'd come too far to ever let a bitch think I was a quitter. Bitches wanted my spot and I wasn't just going to let another have what I worked hard for. Faheem may have been a fuck up but he was my fuck up. Again,

I twirled my engagement ring thinking enough was indeed enough. If I was going to forgive this nigga, I had to set some rules. As I went to unblock his number, I peeped I had a text message from Syncere. It read:

*SYNCERE: Pretty P, I hope yo' day is going well today. I'mma keep you in my prayers. Shit will get better. Trust me on that. Fuck with a nigga.*

A smile crept upon my face as I reread the message a few more times. It seemed so easy to forget the bullshit and start fresh but I knew it could never be that easy. Instead of replying, I unblocked Faheem's number and it was like the nigga knew the exact moment when I did the shit because my phone rang almost immediately. *Triggered* played as I stared at my ringing phone. My head was telling me to ignore it, my pride was screaming FUCK THAT NIGGA but my heart, man, I listened to that bitch every trip.

"Yeah?" I answered.

Faheem sighed into the phone and said, "We gotta get this shit together, P."

"I agree. So what's new?"

"On some real shit, I cannot lose you. I will not lose you. Understand me? I love you, Peyton."

I closed my eyes and sighed once more before replying, "I love you too, Faheem."

# MILAH

The next day rolled around and I turned over in bed feeling lonely and annoyed. Teddy didn't come through last night and I was mad at myself for convincing Peyton's ass to go home to Faheem. The whole time I'm screaming FUCK THAT NIGGA in my head while she poured her problems on me. He cheated on her every chance he got and the shit was sickening. He was slinging dick all over Carol City and then some. Man, fuck him for putting my best friend through the most.

"Niggas ain't shit..." I grumbled as I snatched my bonnet off and reached for the cigarette in the ashtray on my nightstand. I could tell this day wasn't about to go good for me. My phone rang and I wondered why the fuck was she calling me. Sighing, I reluctantly slid the bar to answer the call. I faked a big ass yawn and said, "Yeah hello?"

"Milah, wake up. I'm in big trouble."

I puffed on the cigarette and blew the smoke out as I ran my fingers through my hair. "What happened?"

On the other end of the phone, my nineteen year old cousin Chiquita sobbed into the phone.

"I'm pregnant again and my mama done kicked me out. I needa come stay with you for a lil' while." she explained.

"Wait, what?" I raised my eyebrow and looked at the phone in confusion. "Girl, you better hit up yo' baby daddy. What the hell?"

"Hell nah!" Quita shouted. "This muthafucka on some other shit. It's looking like I'm in this alone. What the fuck am I gonna do, Milah?"

She started crying loudly into the phone and I had to ask myself the same question. What the fuck was she gon' do? She wasn't staying with me. Quita came with too much baggage and was always fucking pregnant. I remember the first time she found out she was pregnant with twins. She came to me lookin for advice like my ass would know what to do with a baby right now. I told her to ask the nigga she was fucking for some abortion money and get rid of the kid.

Sure enough, Quita didn't listen and ended up a single mother at sixteen years old. Struggling with twins, I assumed she would have learned but nope, here she was knocked up again and crying to me. The situation seemed familar and her mother clearly wasn't playing that shit having three babies in the crib. While I felt a lil' bad, I really didn't have any words for her.

"Um, hello?" Quita called out to me, snapping me back to the conversation. "I need your fucking help and you're just on mute! What's good with that?"

"I'm fucking thinking, Quita. Goddamn!" I yelled. Another call came through but I ignored it and hopped off my bed. I paced my bedroom floor and put the phone on speaker. "It's gon' be alright."

"Okay but when? Milah, I'm-"

I pinched the bridge of my nose and let out a frustrated groan when the same number called back. I had to get up off this damn phone. "Aight Quita, just gimme a day or two to figure some shit out."

"Are you sure? 'Cause..."

"Yes, I'll hit you back!" I angrily shouted into the phone before clicking over. "Yeah, who's this?"

"Damn, it's nice to hear yo' voice too," Teddy mumbled. "Come to Mercy, a nigga been hit up."

"What? When? What happened?"

"Can't say too much but come see me right now. My mother bouta dip and I want you by my side."

"I'm on my way." Hearing his voice, I knew he was all fucked up and it brought tears to my eyes. I kind of liked Teddy's ass and to know he thought that much of me to call at this time meant something to me. I couldn't believe what he was saying. I rushed to shower, get dressed and headed to the hospital to see him.

When I got there, I made my way to the information desk when I overheard some nigga was speaking to a nurse about Teddy. Walking over to them, I interrupted the conversation by clearing my throat. "Excuse me, y'all talking about Theodore Stephens? I'm his girl, Milah."

The dude eyeballed me up and down like he doubted that shit and questioned, "Who are you?"

Rolling my eyes, I replied, "I just told you. He called me and told me to come up here to see him." Turning to look at the nurse, I asked, "Is he okay? Where's his room?"

The nurse looked at the dude then back at me before he just shook his head and thanked the nurse for al of her help. He looked me up and down and said, "Milah, how come I ain't never heard of you? I mean, you could be up here on some OPPS shit."

"Look, whoever *you* are, I said what the fuck I said. I'm Milah, Teddy's girl. Now, where is he?" This ignorant ass muthafucka didn't say shit to me, he just walked off down the hall but I surely did follow. Before walking in the room, he said, "If you ain't welcome, you gotta go. Sorry."

I scoffed and pushed past him to get to Teddy. "Damn boo, I'm so sorry." I rushed to his bedside and kissed all over his face. Smirking over in homeboy's direction, I noticed he was genuinely shocked to see I was Teddy's girl. I didn't even peep this older woman in the room and I no longer cared about the nigga with the attitude. I just cared that my meal ticket was alive and breathing.

# SYNCERE

Whoever this Milah bitch was, I didn't like her ass already but it wasn't the time to get into all that right now. While this nigga Teddy was in emergency surgery with my aunt by his side, I went out to Cypress Grove to Nina's crib. Sure enough, she had about two kilos of heroin, five ounces of weed, a couple vials of coke, and two semi-automatics. I instantly got hot as fuck because that's exactly how I got booked for years. This nigga Teddy had to be dumb as hell to be having all this shit on him. I took it all from Nina and assured her I would find out who shot my cousin. I demanded that she lay low and if she needed anything just to call me.

Now here I sat with this nigga still in the hospital and my aunt looked drained. Since Teddy was rushed to the hospital, she was right there. He was shot a total of six times. Whoever ran down on my cousin intended for him to die in cold blood yesterday. Either it wasn't his time to go or he was built Ford Tough. After a great debate with the board and the best fucking surgeon at Mercy Hospital, his ass underwent major surgery.

"I'm just glad to be live, cuh," Teddy spoke. "A nigga could be-"

"Uh uh, don't you dare say it." Aunt Jackie interjected and stood up by his bedside holding a bible. She shook her head and continue, "God will never leave you nor forsake you. You hear me?" She closed her eyes as she placed her hand on his chest.

"Exactly boo. God don't make no mistakes and you're here for a reason" Milah smiled at him and rubbed her growing belly.

Frowning, I said, "Just know you gon' be straight, cuh." I pounded my chest.

He slowly nodded his head as he held his mother's hand. "Where's these niggas at?" He asked, referring to Faheem and Saige.

"Business." I shrugged my shoulders then said, "But best believe that nigga Heem been hitting me up to check on yo' progress and shit. He said he got you as soon as you get out and get back to yo' normal wild boy ass." Milah and I laughed while my aunt went off.

"Like hell you are!" She lashed out and cut her eyes at me before moving closer to Teddy. "That bastard don't mean you no good. If I catch you still playing around with yo' life, Teddy Lewis, so help me God, I will be the one to take you out this muthafucka!" She checked him like she meant business.

Teddy locked eyes with his mother then

looked at me and finally his eyes landed back on his mother. He licked his lips and replied, "Don't know what to tell you, mama. I'mma thug 'til I die. Ain't shit changed but the fucking day."

I shrugged my shoulders and added, "Auntie, no disrespect but whoever did this will be dealt with and that's a big fact."

"I hear that. And Teddy..."

"Lil' girl, ain't nobody talking to you! And you two, are hardheaded negros who make me sick!" Aunt Jackie snatched up her purse with the matching leather jacket and stormed off. "Retaliation leads to death! Just ask your father, Teddy. Oops, you can't because he's dead!" She left the room in a rage.

Milah kissed his cheek. "It's gon' be alright, boo. Handle yo' business."

"You already know that, shawty. Fuck what my mam think, I'mma grown ass man over here." His mind was made up and I couldn't say I blamed him. But he didn't have to worry about shit. I was determined to dead the muthafuckas who tried to kill my cousin.

\*\*\*

Hours later, I was finally getting to the crib. First thing I did was hop in the shower then twist up a fat ass. Shit was much needed. Laying back with my eyes closed just thinking Pretty P slipped into my thoughts again. I wondered what her sexy ass was doing since she wasn't fucking with me. She'd been avoiding my texts for a few days now. I was annoyed but at the same time, I was also worried. I decided to call her this time instead of sending a text. Imagine my surprise when she answered on the second ring.

"Hello?"

"Well, damn, if it isn't Miss MIA," I joked with her, all puns intended. "What's good with ya? You good?"

"Ummm, who is this? You also been texting my phone like you know me too."

"Don't be getting crazy. You know damn well who this is." I looked at my phone to be sure I had the right number. "Damn, a nigga saves yo' life and you forget about my ass? That's fucked up, P." She started cracking up laughing.

"Ohhh... this must be, ummm Syncere, huh?"

"Better recognize and don't let that shit happen again." I hit the blunt and exhaled.

"Boy, bye. I just copped the newest iPhone and some shit happened where I lost all my contacts so nope, your number wasn't saved," P explained.

"Well, save that shit now." I demanded then heard background noises and she told someone to have a good night. As a cash register sounded off, I asked, "Oh, my fault. Did I catch you at the store or something?"

"Not *the* store but *my* store, yes." She so humbly responded. "It's cool though. I'm actually closing up as we speak."

"Check you the fuck out, big shot." I laid back on my pillows because a nigga was actually enjoying this lil' conversation. "You a store owner, P?"

"Yeah. I own three boutiques in Miami and I'm considering opening a fourth if I can get it together."

"I feel that. Congrats, baby. You independent, feisty and sexy as fuck? Please tell me more."

P laughed again. Damn her shit was sexy. She said, "You know damn well you don't wanna hear about my businesses. You just tryna get up in these lace panties. Game recognize game, Syncere."

"Game?" I questioned. "You ain't even seen no game, man. This is me all day and the next. I wanna get to know you better. I mean, I wanna know everything from yo' deepest fears to yo' wildest dreams." I told her. I hit the blunt and exhaled before continuing, "I wanna know what makes you sad, what can make you happy and what yo' ass is generally all about. I wanna know you, P. For real. So, it's either you let a nigga in or I'mma just kidnap you and hold you hostage until you let me love you."

We both laughed at that and then she got quiet on me. I could tell she was thinking about what I'd just said, and truth be told, I was too. I'd never wanted a female so much in my life. I wanted her badly. I had to have her. After a few moments of silence, P finally responded.

"You wanna know all that, huh? Like, on the real?"

"Just give a nigga a smoke signal or something and I'mma come with my cape and snatch yo' ass up from that weak ass nigga. You really too beautiful of a person to be settling. Believe that." I finished the blunt and then buried myself up under the covers. Shorty had me feeling all weird inside. This shit wasn't me at all. I felt like a lil' nigga sneaking to talk on the phone under the covers back in day.

"See, you mentioned the fact that I have a nigga already. So..." I heard doors closings and keys jingling in the background.

"So, you can cut the bullshit right here. Whoever yo' nigga is, is seriously slacking. That shit is clear as fucking day. So, I'm saying though, why not put yo'self in the presence of a real Carol

City nigga? What's the harm in a friendly outing? Just you and me." P's ass had me open off basic conversation but I was rolling with it. "I know you feeling a nigga and you know I'm on yo' back. You just scared to step outside yo' comfort zone. Is that it?" I continued to press the issue and she just sighed heavily.

"Look, that's my other line beeping. I'mma save your number in this new phone and maybe I'll be at Ball & Chain jazz club one Saturday night. Who knows?" She whispered into the phone. "I might see you there." I caught the hint and threw her the confirmation.

"Oh, you'll definitely see me there one night. You gon' take a long walk on the beach with me when that shit let out?" I laughed but I was dead serious. She laughed back.

Laughing back, she said, "Goodnight, Syncere."

"Aight, Pretty P. You have a good night as well."

# FAHEEM

"Who you on the phone all cheesy with like that?"

I stepped inside Radiance ready to scoop Peyton for our date and noticed she was smiling like a muthafucka. I figured it would be nice to have a lil' date night for once; dinner, a movie and some crazy ass sex. Peyton tossed on her jean jacket and locked her office door.

"Oh, hey. You're actually on time, huh?" She grinned at me while she twitched her sexy ass over to where I stood . Kissing my lips, she said, "That was just Milah's crazy ass. Come on, I'm starving."

I licked my lips, looking her up and down and replied, "Me too, lemme eat yo' pussy from the back real quick." She broke out laughing but I was serious. Her ass was sitting in that jean romper and P had a mean shoe game. Shit, I was damn near drooling.

Peyton swatted my chest and said, "Boy, bye. Now come on, I'm ready to eat." She hit the lights, opened the door and pulled me behind her. I grimaced. A nigga was horny as fuck! Since we had made up and come to terms with our relationship a few days ago, we hadn't fucked at all. She ain't even suck a nigga's dick. I was fiending for some pussy and hoping she stopped being stubborn and give me what was mine.

We headed for Barracudas Seafood and Grill. I gripped her thigh and decided to see what was up with us fucking at the end of the night. "Baby, when you gon' let a nigga out the doghouse? I think I've been a good boy. What's good?"

She laughed, waved her finger *'no'* and responded, "You been good for like four days, Heem, and that don't mean shit. But," She leaned over to finger my beard. "Let's see how the night goes and I might put this pretty pussy on you." She winked and I sucked my teeth.

"Man, you bullshitting. It's been forever, P. I need to feel that pussy, baby." I told her, feeling annoyed. Damn, I felt like I was begging for what was already mine.

"And I need to feel appreciated and secure so..." She rolled her neck.

My phone rang I peeped it was, my baby's mother, Faye, calling me. I hit the ignore button to continue the conversation with Peyton. I understood where she was coming from but at the same time, she didn't want me fucking other bitches so why not just fuck me? Why play these mind games?

"I hear you, P. I do and I'mma show and prove but in the meantime between time, yo' nigga got needs and I needs that pussy." I slid my hand between her thighs and my dick got hard immediately when I felt her warmth. The sound of my phone going off again interrupted everything. "Fuck man!" I was annoyed. Peyton moved my hand and leaned closer to the passenger door to eyeball me.

"Uh huh, that's probably a bitch blowing you up right now. What's fucking new?"

"Watch yo' mouth. It's Saraj's mama calling me. Hold on." I finally answered the call and all I heard was my daughter crying in the background.

"Faheem, please come get this lil' jit! Niggas just drove by shooting at the crib next door and Saraj won't stop crying. All she wants is you!" Faye hollered.

"What the fuck? Stop all that yelling 'cause you probably over there getting her all riled up too. What the fuck happened?"

"Oh, you got bitches screaming at you now? Really?" Peyton leaned forward with her fists balled up. I motioned for her to be silent because my baby's mother just wouldn't stop crying on the other end of the phone. All I heard in the background was my chaos and my daughter screaming crying for me.

"I was chilling on the stoop with my home-girls and the kids. Next thing I know, we hear bullets start flying from the crib next door." Faye explained." We ran inside with the kids but Saraj is still flipping the fuck out! Shit is crazy over here and she's crying her ass off for you. Can you come through and get her, man?"

I looked over at Peyton as I pulled my truck in the opposite direction. Her ass was staring back at me with a confused look plastered on her face. "I'm on my way. Did you see what the muthafuckas looked like?"

"A black Audi with some dark ass tints, that's all I could see before I ran in the crib."

"Aight, get her ready." I ended the call and headed to my baby mama's crib. Although I heard my daughter going crazy in the background, I couldn't tell if Faye was saying whatever just to get me to come though or if some shit really did go down. Glancing over at Peyton, I knew she was pissed just from her body language. I went to grip her thigh and she slapped my hand.

"So what Faye need you to come running for now?" She gave me the side eye but once I explained the situation, her ass calmed down somewhat. She was hot about our date night getting cut short but, at the same time, P was understanding as fuck. Man, Saraj was my baby girl. I was always there.

We pulled up to Faye's in like twenty minutes and just like she said, her area was crazy hot. It looked like a scene from First 48 with a bunch of cops asking questions nobody was going to answer. Leaving my gun in the car with Peyton, I hopped out and tried to walk through the crowd.

"And who the fuck are you?" One of the cops asked with his hand on his gun. I wished a muthafucka would. I gritted my teeth and started to say something slick when I heard Faye's voice.

"Let him through! That's my daughter's father! Excuse me, excuse me." She came over rolling her neck giving the officer much attitude. A nigga really didn't need the extra attention. She tried linking arms with me and I pulled away. "Well, damn, hello to you too, Faheem."

"Daddy! Daddy!" Saraj came running over and jumped into my arms all excited but I could tell she had really been crying. Her hazel eyes were all red and puffy so I kissed all over her face to make her giggle.

"That's daddy's baby. You okay?" She nodded her head and I smiled. "Aight, we out then."

"Wait, so that's it?" Faye asked, yanking on my arm.

"What did you expect? Man, I told you we ain't even on that type of time no more, Faye." I told her with a slight smirk and reached for the

141

small unicorn book bag in her hand. Her ass followed me talking shit as I walked to the car holding Saraj.

"I'm saying though, what yo' bitch in the car or something? I can't get a lil'-"

"Watch yo' mouth for the last time 'bout mine, Faye. For real. I'll bring jit back in a couple days."

Peyton stepped out to help me get Saraj in the back of my whip. Faye's petty ass gon' start some shit by showing off the tattoo on her arm. It was a pretty ass *F* sitting on a crown surrounded by clouds. I forgot she got that shit and she swore up and down that it was for me.

Smirking, she said, "Okay, baby. I'll see you this weekend."

"Bitches always tryna be funny..." Peyton mumbled and closed the back door.

"Man, Faye, carry yo' ass back in the goddamn house! P, get in the truck." My baby's mother walked off waving and giggling and I flipped her annoying ass the finger. Pulling off, I shook my head, "I don't know why you feed into that girl."

"So, you seeing her this weekend, Heem?"

"Peyton, she was talking to Saraj."

"Mmm. I don't know why you had to fuck with that girl, Faheem!" She spoke sarcastically and folded her arms, hot as hell.

I was annoyed myself and instead of arguing over Faye's ass, I turned the music up and blocked everything out. Shit, this wasn't how a nigga's night was supposed to go. I was supposed to be knee deep in some pussy. Glancing over at Peyton in the passenger seat, I smirked to myself. She still looked good as fuck even though she had her mad face on. Nah, I was gon' have to fuck that attitude right out of her.

# CHAPTER SEVEN

# PEYTON

*"Who came to make sweet love? Not me. Who came to kiss and hug? Not me? Who came to beat it up? Rocky. And don't use those hands to put up that gate and stop me. When we...fuck..."*

"Oh, my God..." I moaned as Tank sang through the speakers and arched my back some more. I don't know if it was because we hadn't fucked in a good lil' minute or what, but Faheem was hitting every spot from every angle. He had me face down, ass up and gripping the sheets. "Damn, baby. I'm 'bouta cum again." He snatched me up by my little bit of hair and pressed harder on the small of my back. I screamed in pleasure as he hit my pussy harder and harder. The wetness between my thighs was crazy.

"Go 'head and bust that nut then baby. You deserve it."

"Shiiit, baby!" I closed my eyes and bit down on my top lip. Sweat dripped from him onto my neck. Fuck love making, this nigga was fucking the soul out of me. This shit right here was everything. I shuddered. "That's my ssspotttt..."

Faheem gripped the back of my neck and slammed me face first into the plush mattress. He growled and I loved that shit. "Damn, P. I missed this pussy. You cannot be keeping the goods from me, baby." I clenched my pussy muscles and looked back at him.

"This should be the only pussy you missing, nigga." He slapped my ass cheeks and ran up in me deeper.

"Shut up."

I shivered as I could feel another nut about to rip. I bit the sheets to keep myself from screaming. Saraj was finally sound asleep after fighting it for hours once we got home. Faheem leaned down to suck on my neck and pinch my nipples at the same damn time. He knew that shit drove me over the edge. My nipples were so sensitive that the wind could blow a certain way, and I'd be creaming my panties.

"Mm-hmm, I feel that shit. Cum for daddy."

"Ohh, ohhh, sshhiiiiittt...I'm bouta...I'm bouta..."

"Fuck, Peyton." He gripped my waistline and plunged into my wetness. "You got me 'bouta nut, too. Take all this shit, baby. Fuck!" He groaned loudly as he came then collapsed on top of me, all out of breath. I tried catching my breath my damn self.

"Damn, babe. Them backshots were righteous." I giggled as he nibbled on my earlobe. "I guess I missed your ass too." I couldn't front, no matter what we went through, the sex was always bomb as fuck. I couldn't understand why Faheem would ever stray. I was the full package. Most times though, the sex clouded the bigger picture but for now, I was content. We cuddled up and knocked the hell out.

*** 

Two days later, I found myself pulling up to my parents' house for the first time since that day my daddy died. Paris told me she'd moved back home to keep my mother company and help her cope with daddy's death. It was about three months later and the shit still hurt like hell. I held back the tears that threaten to fall and got myself in check.

"Woosah, P. Just breathe. Just breathe."

I was hoping to get back on the right track with my mother and I definitely missed my older sister. Paris said she had some news to share and invited me over for a mother/daughter luncheon. I exited my truck feeling good. I needed this little outing because for the past two days, I'd been playing mama to Saraj. I rang the bell and a few moments later, Paris opened the door wearing this pretty flowy dress and a huge smile.

"Damn, baby sister. I was wondering when

your ass was gon' get outta the car!" She exclaimed and we both laughed as we stepped inside.

"Leave me alone." The smell of my mother's cooking smacked me in the face. I licked my lip with anticipation and asked, "Damn, mama in here throwing down, huh?"

"Okayyy!" Paris agreed. "I helped with the cornbread though." I started cracking up because she couldn't cook for shit!

"I'm sure you did, sis. Where's mama at anyway?"

"She'll be down in a minute."

We walked into the family room and my heart almost stopped. Where was my daddy's portrait? It always hung above the fireplace my entire life. Where were his gold medals? My eyes shot to the mantel and the only pictures were of Paris and me. All of the family pictures were gone from the living room. I turned to face my sister who had just taken a seat on the couch. That's when I noticed my daddy's favorite lounge chair was gone as well! What the fuck was going on? I glared at Paris, ready for war.

"Where's all of daddy's pictures, Paris? Where are they? Why are they not up?" I questioned.

She shrugged her shoulders and replied,

"Well, Mama was having a hard time, baby sister. She thought it would be best to-"

"Best to get rid of his shit and act like he never fucking existed?" I was pissed and moved closer to my sister, wanting to knock her tall ass out. "You condone that fuckery, Paris? Really?" I couldn't believe what I was seeing and hearing right now.

"Aye, I don't think you oughta be speaking like that in yo' mama's house."

I turned around so fast, a bitch damn near caught whiplash. In the foyer stood, Reverend Watson holding a piece of chicken and a Corona. He wore a pair of tan slacks, a wife beater and his famous alligator shoes.

"Reverend Watson?"

"In the flesh." He took a swig of his beer and walked into family room. Plopping down on the couch across from Paris, he continued, "It's gon' be some changes around here and I think it's best that we all get along." He belched and sighed.

"What the fuck are you talking about?"

Paris sat there twirling her hair with her finger looking dumbfounded. I stormed out of the living room in search of my mother for some clarity on this circus taking place. She definitely had some explaining to do. "Mama, where you at?" I hollered out to her. She wasn't in the kitchen so I stomped up the staircase and burst into her room. I found her standing in the mirrors praying perfume. She was dressed up in rose gold sequins dress, heels and a medium length China bang wig. I'd never seen my mother look like this *ever*. "Mama, why the hell is Reverend Watson downstairs talking like he's replacing my daddy or something? What the fuck is going on?"

She sighed and said, "Well, hello to you too, Peyton," she greeted me. "I thought we could have a nice family afternoon and celebrate. Now, Reverend Watson has been very caring and helpful and-"

I looked my mother up and down and replied, "Helpful to what, your pussy?" *SMACK!*

"You better watch your goddamn mouth! That was twice and I done told you about that." My mother slapped the dog shit out of me but I still didn't hold back.

"Mama, how could you? Daddy ain't been buried but for a hot second and you just up and replace him?!" I held my cheek and glared up at my mother. I was more hurt than a little bit. Tears of anger built up in my eyes and I couldn't hold them shits back any longer. She waved me off and brushed past me like it was nothing.

"Oh, Peyton. Please stop with the dramatics. Your father was my husband and if I can let go then so can you. Now please pull yourself together and let's enjoy lunch and celebrate." She stood in the doorway and looked over her shoulder.

"Celebrate what? You creeping with the reverend?" I rolled my eyes and wiped my tears.

My mother cackled ang replied, "No, silly. Didn't your sister tell you about the baby?"

My heart sank and it felt like I'd been gut punched. My mouth hit the floor and it became hard to breathe. "B-Baby? What ba...mama, what baby?"

Her facial expression turned from glorious to regretful, realizing she'd just fucked up. "Pey, I'm sorry. I assumed she told you..." Paris appeared in the doorway behind my mother holding her belly and I contemplated pushing her ass back down the stairs.

"Baby sister..."

I squinted my eyes and walked closer to the both of them. "So, this is the real reason why we haven't spoken and why you've been shutting me out? Huh? Everybody's keeping secrets in this bitch!" I scoffed and pushed past them. I had to get the fuck away from them.

"It's not like that, Peyton, and you know it."

"Pey," my mother called after me. "Wait a minute. Please!"

"Nah, baby, let her gon' and go now." Reverend Watson snarled at me. "She always was the rebellious one."

"Fuck you, you dirty muthafucka!" I spit in his face.

"You little bitch!" He grasped at my neck and I immediately tried poking his eyes out. He screamed, "Aaaahhhhh!!!"

"Peyton, stop it! Donald, let her go! Oh, my God!"

Paris attacked him from behind. "Get the hell off my sister!"

"Have you all lost your mind?!" My mother shouted and stomped her foot. "Everybody stop it right goddamn now!"

Struggling to breathe, I managed to pull my pocketknife out and slice that holy bastard across his face. Blood splattered everywhere as he let go of me and fell to the ground screaming his head off.

"What have you done?!" My mother shrieked and ran to the reverend's side. She could have cared less that I was coughing up a lung and trying to catch my breath.

With tears in her eyes, Paris helped me up and said, "Just go, baby sister. Please just go."

I shook my head, glanced down at the reverend bleeding and my eyes grew wide. *What the*

153

*fuck did you just do, Peyton?* My heart started pounding and I ran the fuck out of there. I could still hear the reverend screaming and my mother crying out loud asking God why.

Once in the car, I fumbled for my phone as I screeched away from the curb. I called up Milah and her phone just rang. "Come on, best friend. Pick up!" No answer so I called up Faheem and of course his phone went straight to voicemail. "Fucking figures! Shit!" I banged on the steering wheel. I could feel a panic attack coming on. I needed somebody and I needed them now. I bent the corner and then Syncere popped into my head. Quickly, I went to my recent calls and pressed the button. His phone rang a few times and then he picked up.

"Well, if it isn't my future baby mama," he laughed. "Pretty P, what it do?"

"I need you. I'm scared as shit right now." I started hyperventilating and my vision became blurry. I blinked a few times and then had to slam on my breaks to keep from hitting this motor-cycle in front of me at the red light.

"Where you at?" Syncere asked with worry dripping from his voice.

"Ummm..." I looked out the window. "I'm not too far from the Parkland Library." I told him and sniffled into the phone. "I just did some wild shit and I'm...I'm..."

"P, calm down. Gimme twenty minutes. Aight?"

# SYNCERE

"Damn, cuh. You leaving already?" Saige asked as he turned up the Remy bottle and slapped a stripper's ass. "You know the party just getting started!"

"It's hella early." Faheem added then ashed his blunt.

I stepped back into the 'Playa's Room' at Saige's crib after hanging up with P and as tempted as I was to stay at the turn up, I knew she needed me. To know she hit me up instead of her nigga meant something to me and had me wishing I could fly to her ass. These hoes could wait. I dapped these niggas up and replied, "Nah, I'mma let y'all indulge. I got something better waiting on a nigga," I smirked and rubbed my hands together like Birdman.

This nigga Faheem laughed and said, "Fool, you tripping. This is where it's at." *Freak Hoes* popped on and all six strippers started popping hella pussy on the handstand. I looked at a couple doing their thing and he asked me, "You sure about that move, cuh? Bitch must be some kind of special."

"I mean, she ain't no bitch but yeah, she's

special. I'mma link with y'all." I left out and made my way to Parkland. I put the library in my GPS and laughed because Parkland was bougie and I couldn't picture P being from there. She seemed soft enough but also a little rough around the edges, kind of like a chocolate chip cookie. I called her when I was about to turn the corner.

"You still there, right?"

She sighed. "Yeah, I'm here. Where you at?"

I beeped the horn and watched as she looked in her rearview mirror. She hopped out of her Range Rover, locked up then walked over to my whip as I unlocked the door for her to get in. I asked, "You gon' leave yo' shit right there?"

"Yeah, I mean, it *is* Parkland. It should be fine."

My eyes wandered all over her body and noticed she had a little blood splatter on her white tank top and cropped jean jacket. We looked at each other but neither one of us said a word. She took her jacket off and balled it up. I took her hand in mine and pulled off. After a few moments of silence, I finally spoke.

"So, what's good? Talk to me. Why you got blood on you?"

P sighed and placed her head against the headrest before she replied, "I just sliced the Reverend from my family's church."

Glancing over at her, I laughed but stopped when I saw she was so serious. "What the fuck? What happened?" I questioned.

Sighing heavily she responded, "I don't even know where to begin. You might not understand and-"

I pressed. "Try me. I like to think I'm a very understanding person. Talk to me."

P paused then said, "What would you do if you felt like everyone around you is causing pain or confusion? What would do you if you felt like you had nothing left to give? Like, you're an overly squeezed lemon and folks just keep on squeezing you and squeezing you to the point where you feel used up and worthless? Like there's nothing left." She glanced over at me.

I kept my eyes on the road but I could hear the frustration and sadness in her tone and I wanted to hug her so badly. Before I could speak, she continued. "I'm frustrated with my love life, I just buried my father a few months back, I think my best friend doesn't really have my best interest at heart and now I'm beefing with my mom and my sister." She started crying then out of nowhere, blurted out, "Yo', just pull over! This was a mistake. I don't know you and I'm just venting all my problems. Pull over!" P yelled.

I looked at her like she was crazy because she was if she thought she was getting away from me now. Fuck that, I kept driving. Next thing I knew, the passenger door swung open and her ass was getting ready to jump out. "Aye!" I swerved as I grabbed onto her arm.

"Let me go!" P cried. "I just wanna run away! Let...me...go!"

"Are you fucking crazy?" I skillfully switched lanes and pulled over. Pulling her into me, I closed the door and hugged her close. She sobbed into my chest. "Damn, you can't be doing this shit. What type of shit you on?"

Pulling away from me, she pounded on my chest. "Oh, like you ain't never been going through something and wanted to run away from it all? How dare you fucking judge me?!"

"I just spent eight years locked behind the wall, so trust me, I done been through some shit! Aight?" I held her wrists and we locked eyes and I could see her emotions were written all over her face. "I'm not here to judge you at all. You called me for help and a nigga really wanna be here for you."

The tears ran down P's face as she looked deep into my eyes and said, "I've really been the best bitch I know how to be. Why doesn't he love me?"

"He's a bitch. That's why I was sent to you. Just let me love you."

When I said that shit, it looked like she was about to overflow with tears any minute. I couldn't help myself. I had to kiss her. We gazed at each other as I brought her lips to mine. They were soft as shit just as I imagined them to be. Surprisingly, she slipped her tongue into my mouth and we tongue wrestled for a few moments before she slightly pulled away from me. I licked her lips.

With labored breathing and her lips still against, P whispered, "I just wanna feel better. You know what I mean?" She bit her bottom lip. Lust was all over her face and took the hint

"I know exactly what you need, beautiful." I hit the button on the side of the passenger seat to lay the entire seat down and shifted it backwards. Thank God for tinted windows because I was about to get my feast on. My hands reached for the zipper on her jeans, but my eyes never left hers. Out of nowhere, P attacked me and started kissing me like she needed me. I could feel the heat radiating from her body. "Lay back." I told her. The look in her eye spoke her every emotion. She was in heat and I planned on putting that shit out.

She allowed me to unzip her jeans and I slid them off. I noticed she had a butterfly tattoo on her upper thigh close to her panty line. With the passenger seat pushed damn near in the back seat,

I was able to get between her legs with ease. I sucked between her trembling thighs and kissed my way up to her pussy. No bullshit she smelled good as fuck. My mouth watered as she caressed the back of my head.

"You better know what you're doing down there," P stated jokingly as she closed her eyes. I didn't even say shit back to her. I simply ripped her lace panties off and threw her legs up over my shoulders. The conversation was over.

# FAHEEM

*"Cold sweats (sweaty sheets) from bad dreams (nightmares). I hope the Feds don't grab the team 'cause we been labeled as the troublemakers... DIPSET!"* I bobbed my head and rapped along to some throwback Jim Jones. Swerving on the highway, I was drunk out of my mind and on my way home.

After getting my dick sucked by one of the stripper bitches at Saige's crib, I was more than ready to dive in some pussy. I kept blowing Peyton's phone up but after a few rings, it always went to voicemail. I just assumed her ass was knocked out in our bed waiting for me. Shit, her ass better had be home. It was damn near two in the morning. I was thankful I was able to drop Sarah off to her mama finally after two whole days. A nigga just wanted to feel some pussy in peace and take my ass to sleep.

"If it ain't one thing, it's..."

I instantly got hot when I noticed Peyton's car wasn't parked in the driveway. Pulling into my spot, I grabbed my cell to call her once again. The phone just rang and rang. I called her back to back to back as I stumbled my way into the crib we shared. It was dark as shit without a trace of her being there. "Aye, where the fuck are you at and why ain't yo' ass home in my fucking bed?" I barked into the phone, leaving her a voicemail. P ain't never pulled no shit like this before. Still in the dark, I plopped down on the couch staring at the front door hot like a muthafucka. I turned up the Remy bottle and kept drinking as I continued to blow her phone up until I eventually passed out.

***

The sound of something jingling and then hitting the floor woke me out of my slumber. I quickly reached for my glock on the couch next to me and aimed it at the figure in front of me. Squinting my eyes, I peeped it was Peyton finally making her appearance. The sun had come up and was shining through the blinds. Who the fuck did she think she was to be coming home with the sun? She had me fucked up.

She threw her hands up and whispered, "Baby, it's just me."

"Name one reason I shouldn't pull this fucking trigger right now, Peyton." Seeing red, I cocked my gun back and walked towards her. I watched as her eyes grew wider and wider while she backed into the front door. She stood frozen in place with fear written all over her face. "You think I won't kill you, P? Huh?" I pressed up against her and held the gun to her temple while she squirmed to get

163

away

"What the fuck are you doing, Faheem? Stop it! You're drunk. Move!"

I let off a single shot towards the ceiling and she screamed and tried to run past me. I slapped her ass back and she dropped to the floor. Standing over her, I yelled, "You fucking someone else, P?! Huh? I been calling yo' ass, blowing yo' shit up and you gon' walk up in here talking 'bout some 'baby, it's me'? Bitch, you got me fucked up!" I grabbed Peyton by the throat to sit her up. Her left eye was red and the mascara she wore started running down her face.

She cried out, "I was at my fucking moms!"

"Bullshit! Call her!" I rebutted.

"What?"

"I said call yo' mama. I'm not fucking playing with you!" I gripped the back of her neck and pushed her towards the couch. "Sit down and call her, Peyton." I demanded and wiped the spit from my lips. I felt like a fucking mad man on a wild rampage in this bitch. Did she really come home at six something in the morning thinking that shit was cool? I aimed my gun at her.

Peyton held her head and screamed, "You're fucking drunk! Stop doing this! I was just at my fucking mother's house!"

I lowered my gun and squinted my eyes at my fiancé again only this time my eyes zeroed in on her hand. I noticed she wasn't wearing her ring and I fucking lost it. Something came over me when I punched her right in her lying ass face. Blood immediately erupted from her nose. I didn't give a fuck though. I punched her twice more and then dragged her screaming ass off the couch. "P, you got me fucked up right now." I told her.

"Let me go! Please stop it!!! Baby, stop!!! Please!!!" She kicked and screamed as I held her wrists and dragged her up the stairs to the bathroom.

"Please what? Stop what? Was you telling that nigga to stop when he was fucking the shit out of you?" I kicked her in the side of the head.

Gasping for air, I jumped out of my sleep, dripping sweat and alarming the female who was passed out in my lap. My heart was beating dumb fast as I took a look around. I realized I was still in my brother's crib. Trap music played low on the plasmas hanging on the wall. There were empty Henny and D'Ussé bottles on the floor along with food and single dollar bills. Blinking a few times, I shook that crazy ass dream off, but my gut was telling me to get my drunk ass home. The stripper bitch wiped the corners of her mouth and yawned.

"Mmmm, see, I told you my head game is so good it'll knock you out." She winked at me.

I shook my head and ignored her remark. For some reason, I felt sick to my stomach. I didn't know if it was all the L I had consumed throughout the day catching up to me or that wild ass dream of me beating P's ass. It could have been a combination of both. Shit, all I knew was I had to stop fucking around on my baby 'cause clearly I'd lose my damn mind if I found out the tables had turned. I handed ol' girl another hundred dollar bill, thanked her for the bomb head and dipped. On the way out, she had the nerve to ask me for a ride home since she told her girls she was good with me for the night. In my book, the night was over. Fuck that. I was going home to my bitch. Plus, I didn't give hoes rides unless I was benefiting from it. I got what I wanted from her already. Fuck she thought.

# CHAPTER
# EIGHT

# PEYTON

You know that feeling you get when you've done something that probably wasn't the right thing to do but in the heat of the moment, you just didn't give a fuck? You didn't care about the possible consequences to come? You keep asking yourself, how could something so wrong feel so damn right? As I drove along the highway, I wasn't thinking about Faheem and what he would do or how he would feel. Nah, he never crossed my mind. My entire body and mind were at ease and the shit felt so fucking good. Although my pussy yearned for more, I was content with the current status. And for the life of me, I just couldn't get Syncere off my mind.

From the very beginning of him actually answering my distress call to sucking the soul out of my pussy to the deep conversations. He was everything. We spent the whole day together and I actually felt appreciated for once. A smile crept on my face the second I heard Tamar Braxton's *All the Way Home* cut on Pandora. I still loved this song and I was definitely going to be thinking about this shit all the way home. I hoped I dreamt about Syncere too. It was crazy for me to even be feeling this way. Throughout the day, I told myself not to like him but it was too hard. It just felt right.

We ended up at Bahama Grill in Parkland. Over bomb drinks and good food, we talked and talked and talked some more. It was refreshing to pick someone's brain. I learned about his gun and drug conviction and how he spent eight long years behind the wall for taking the wrap for his cousin. Real nigga shit. I respected it and the shit turned me on.

He told me about his upbringing and being raised by his hardworking aunt. He didn't even have to tell me about his current lifestyle. I could tell by the way he spoke, his swag and his whole persona that he moved weight. I never heard of him before but that was a good thing. He was single with no kids, which was most definitely a shocker. I just knew someone had to have trapped his fine ass. The more he shared with me, the more attracted to him I became. Butterflies stayed in my stomach as we gazed into each other's eyes during the whole conversation. It was like he was speaking to my soul.

Syncere made me feel comfortable enough to open up about everything from my childhood and being a daddy's girl, to my emotionally abusive relationship with Faheem, to my dad's death, to my miscarriage and finally my wave of uncertainty with Milah lately. He told me I was stronger than I gave myself credit for and that shit had to change. He assured me he would be there every step of the way despite this fat ass ring on my finger. I knew it would be hard to shake him. This feeling was unlike any other. A part of me was saying, "P, you know better". We walked hand in hand like we I didn't have a care in the world. I wasn't worried about Faheem's bullshit nor was I wasn't thinking about my mama and her fuckery with the Reverend. Syncere made me feel free.

When I pulled up to the house, I wasn't surprised or angry to not see Faheem's truck parked in the driveway. It was only two in the morning and for his ass, that was kind of early to end his night. Suddenly, this wave of fear washed over me as I realized I probably had the scent of another nigga all over me. I threw my truck park, hopped it and flew into the house.

With the blazing water splashing down on me, I toyed with my pussy with Syncere on my mind. Damn, here I go again. What attracted me most about him was he didn't judge me off this weird mental state I was in plus he was a thug and gentleman at the same damn time. I loved that shit. I creamed all over my gel manicured fingers and reminded myself not to fall for this nigga as I replayed the day's events.

*In the front seat of his Navigator, I held the back of his head. When Syncere snatched my panties off and threw my legs up on his shoulders in one swift move, I knew my pussy was in trouble. He didn't say anything as he kissed my pussy and parted the lips with his warm tongue. Sucking on my clit with finesse ever so gently, he made tiny circles with a little pressed added.*

*"Mmmm... damn..."*

*I moaned and held his head in place for a moment. I could get used to this, I thought. Shit, Faheem barely ate my pussy. Only time was when he used it as a tool to shut me up from "complaining" about something. The sensation I was feeling was indescribable. The combination of Syncere's tongue and full lips giving my pussy kisses made me arch my back even more. I let him taste all this pussy. My breathing became shaky as my legs began to tremble. He firmly held me in place as I squirmed away from his tongue. He lifted me up a little bit and put his mouth all in it as I attempted to push his head away. I felt this pressure in my abdomen and I knew what was coming. "Shiiiiit...what are you doing to me?" He lapped at my juices with expertise as I rained all over his tongue. This nigga had me moaning and shaking like a fiend. I kept my eyes closed because I was scared as hell to open them shits up to look at him. A bitch might have fell in love. Syncere kissed the inside of my quivering thighs and softly blew on my pussy.*

*Sitting up, he moved back in the driver's seat and licked his lips. Caressing my thigh, he finally*

171

spoke. "Now that my appetite is well cured, shall we get yo' crazy ass something to eat?" He laughed. I slowly opened my eyes and stared at him with a slight smirk.

"Okay, smart ass. I know of a spot about five minutes from here."

"Baby!"

I heard someone yell and knew it was Faheem coming home. My heart started pounding as my train of thought focused back on the current situation. I needed to get out of the shower. How the hell was I going to explain me showering at two-thirty in the damn morning? Stepping out of the hot water, I wiped the steam from the mirror and smirked at myself. In that moment, I was again carefree. Whatever excuse came to my mind is what I was going to say. Fuck it, let's see how them tables turned.

"Peyton!" He shouted again and this time his voice was much closer. I rolled my eyes because I could hear the drunkenness in his tone of voice. I opened the bathroom door just in time to see him stumble down the hallway. I didn't even have a chance to speak before he covered my lips with his and pressed me up against the wall. We shared a deep, passionate yet sloppy kiss as he dropped my towel to the floor and hugged me close. "Baby, I fucking love you," he said to me as tears rained down his cheeks. "I swear to God, I'll lose my fucking mind if I lose you to the next muthafucka, P. On God!" Faheem cupped my face and kissed me again.

He was scaring the shit out of me. I'd just had a bomb ass day with another nigga and here this one comes in with this shit. Does he know something? Shit! Did he see me pull up? Inside, I was freaking out but I kept it cool. "I love you too, Heem." I caressed the back of his head. "What's wrong?"

He dropped to his knees and placed his hands on my belly. He looked up at me and shook his head before replying, "I'm so sorry about the baby. I think about the shit every fucking day. I'm sorry I keep you so stressed out. Don't fuck with no other nigga, P. I love you, baby. I'll lose my fucking mind if I lose you. You hear me?"

I was so overwhelmed and thrown off by his emotions because this nigga hardly ever cried. He was truly in fare form at the moment and I was taken aback. Being that I just did let a nigga feast on my goodies and make me feel good, I couldn't do shit else but smile and say, "It's okay, baby. I'm here. Get up, please. Stop crying." I told him as I tugged on his button up.

He didn't even reply. He simply lifted me up onto his shoulders and started feasting on my pussy right there in the hallway. I gasped as he skillfully and passionately made love to my already semi swollen clit. I prayed to God Faheem didn't notice because Syncere really did his thing. *Lord if you love me, get me through this one.* I silently prayed as I closed my eyes and enjoyed the head.

As Faheem lay asleep beside me snoring his ass off, I started to doze off my damn self when I received a text from Paris. Sucking my teeth, I blocked her then placed my phone on the night-stand and rolled back over. I hadn't spoken to her since I sliced the reverend that day and she 'announced' her pregnancy. Everything in me was saying *fuck her*. I just wasn't ready to talk to her ass.

# MILAH

"Mmmm, I love this big ass dick!"

"So, go 'head and cum all over this shit." *SLAP!* "What you waiting for?"

"Damn baby, that's my spot too! Shiiiiit..." *SLAP!*

"Mmhmm... cum all on this dick for Daddy."

"Oh, ohhh... shiiiiit..."

*RING RING RING RING RING!!!*

"Hold up, it's my cousin."

"Hold up? Oh, hell nah. Not right now!"

*RING RING RING RING RING!!!*

"Shit! Gimme a second."

I felt Teddy pull his long, thick dick out of my wet pussy and push me off him. I looked over at him like he was fucking crazy. How the fuck can you go from having wild ass sex, about to bust a big ass nut and you jump out the pussy to answer the phone? I wrapped myself up in the sheets and glared at him. This nigga was released from the hospital and recovering well for the last two days. All he talked about was me creaming on his dick

175

and now that the time was coming, his ass was ruining the mood for a fucking phone call. Words couldn't describe my level of anger at that moment.

"What it do, cuh?" Teddy spoke into the phone as he stood by the dresser with his hard dick still gleaming from my wetness.

Squinting my eyes at him, I asked, "Are you serious right now? It better be life or fucking death." He put his hand up to silence me but continued his phone conversation. He mentioned something about leaving for the weekend and I lashed out. "Oh, you ain't going nowhere!" I yelled. Flipping my weave over my shoulders, I reached in the ashtray on the nightstand to spark up the half of cigarette. He had me hotter than a bitch right now! Whenever that bitch nigga Faheem called or his moody ass cousin, he always went running. I understood the whole business first bullshit but damn, sometimes the shit was overly annoying. My pussy was still dripping and waiting to be finished off. Shaking my head, I mumbled under my breath, "I can't believe this muthafucka..."

Teddy stroked his dick while shaking his head. Sighing into the phone, he said, "Gimme a few. I'm like a half away."

"Nigga-" I started to go off but quickly shut the fuck up. Teddy reached for his gun off the dresser and aimed it at me with a look I didn't ever want to see again.

"I got you, cuh. One hunnid." He ended the call and stalked over to me with his 9mm still in his hand. Sitting on the bed in front of me, he snatched the cigarette and put it out then glared at me. He said, "You realize I'm the one taking care of you right now? Hmm?" I cut my eyes at him and didn't say shit. He continued, "When the money or business calls, I answer it. Period. I shouldn't even have to explain that shit to you."

"I was mid nut. Whatever that nigga needed or wanted coulda waited ten minutes. Period! Every time one of them niggas call, you go running like some bitch or something. I'm tired of it. Your cousin got a nasty ass attitude and Faheem always think he's running shit," I vented and probably a little too much of my emotions came pouring out. Without hesitation, Teddy slapped the shit out of me then climbed on top of me. He shoved his gun into my mouth and held me by the throat. My eyes grew wide with fear as I squirmed beneath him.

"Yeah, you ain't got no slick shit to say now, huh? You fucking talk too much for a bitch who does very little. You oughta be sucking this nut outta me so I can hit these streets to do what I do best. Who else kicking you down dough like me? Who else paying yo' bills? Who else dicking you down with this long dick all the time? There's a time and place to speak up and watch how you say that shit. Now, are we fucking clear?" I quickly nodded my head in agreement as a single tear escaped my eye. Teddy eyeballed me one more time before letting go of my neck and climbing off of me. "Now come suck my dick please so I can get the fuck up outta here." He reached for the blunt on the nightstand, sparked it and laid backwards on my bed with the gun in the other hand.

I didn't want to suck shit right now. I contemplated biting his dick and running but I was really kidding myself? I sucked this niggas dick until he disrespectfully busted all over my face. Teddy went to shower and I wiped my face as tears poured from my eyes. I was hot as fuck thinking I had to humble his ass. He got out of the shower and came back in his room to get dressed. I was scrolling on my phone not paying him any attention.

Teddy got dressed, checked under the bed and of course his damn phone started ringing again. He hopped up to leave and kissed my forehead before tossing a couple of bands on the dresser. "Make sure you lock the door when you leave, aight?" Answering the phone as he left out the room, he told the person, "Yeah, I'm on my way."

I waited until I heard the door slam downstairs before jumping out the bed. I let out a huge scream as I held my head. I hated how much I relied on a nigga. I fucking hated it. But what else could I do? I felt stuck because I knew the type of shit I liked to buy I could never afford off of a regular salary. "Damn!" I kicked my foot out and rammed it right into the safe under the bed. Grabbing my foot, I hollered out and started hopping around Teddy's room like a damn fool. That's when I noticed the safe was left open.

See, his ass was in such a hurry to leave and he got caught lacking. An evil smirk appeared on my face just as a thought came to mind. My heart started beating fast and my mouth got watery as shit. Paranoid, I took a quick look around the room and then pulled out the black safe. Inside, there were stacks and stacks of money along with a thick ass gold chain staring me in the face. "Fuck it." I said to myself and quickly emptied the shit into a bag I snatched from Teddy's closet. A bitch literally taking everything. Shit, this muthafucka wanted to disrespect me like I was some nobody ass bitch all of a sudden. The petty in me took over and I no longer gave a fuck.

By the time he would get back to his crib, I'd be long gone. Hell, I could use a vacation anyway. Plus, I told Quita I'd have some way to help her out in a few days and this here lil' come up was looking like a start to something. I quickly threw on my clothes and got the fuck up out of Teddy's crib. Once I made it to my car, I screeched off. It was a little after ten in the morning and here I was speeding through the streets like a mad woman. I had hella bands on me. This was the most money I'd ever seen up close and personal and it was in my possession. I was trying to get the fuck up out of dodge.

I figured I'd give my cousin some money then keep the rest along with the jewelry and possibly start fresh somewhere else. Miami wasn't shit. Why not move someplace else and restart my life? New look, new crib, new wardrobe and snag me a whole new boss nigga. I smiled at the thought of reinventing myself. It sounded like a whole mood to me. The only thing bittersweet was I'd me missing my best friend. I couldn't even tell her about the fuck shit that I'd just done. I just had to tell her I wouldn't be around for a while. Thinking of a quick lie, I called up Peyton.

"Well hello, stranger. To what do I owe this pleasure?"

Laughing, I said, "Bitch, I ain't no stranger. Cut the shit."

"Uh huh. Bitches get some consistent dick and go MIA on their best friends. I see you, boo."

"Not even. Well, actually we both been boo loving, huh? Since you and Faheem made up a few weeks ago, I've barely seen your ass either."

"Yeah, I guess. I been dealing with a lot."

"I feel that," I sighed as I pulled up to a red light. "Well, I was calling because I'm leaving Miami for a little bit. My cousin needs some help taking care of her kids and you know since I ain't doing shit else down here, I agreed to go help out for a couple months. She just moved to Atlanta and shit." I halfway lied.

"Girl, what? You just leaving like that?" Peyton sucked her teeth and asked, "Damn girl, do I get a goodbye lunch or hug or something?"

"I'm on my way to the airport now, P. It was kind of a last minute but spur of the moment type of thing. I'll be back." I chuckled to kind of lighten the mood but the awkwardness could be felt all through the conversation now.

"Millz, I know you. Everything alright?"

"Yeah, I told you-"

"I know what you told me but you don't even sound right. Talk to me. Matter fact, where you at?"

"Peyton, I gotta go! I'll call you."

"Milah-"

I hung up on her and immediately hit up Chiquita. "Hey, get dressed. I'm getting ready to come scoop you."

"Bet."

"Aight listen, you might not like this but you gon' have to call up Unk. I think a bitch got a plan."

# SYNCERE

"What it do, Auntie? You aight?"

"I'm doing alright, baby."

"I smell them yams on the stove. Lemme get a lil' sample," I laughed as I greeted my aunt with a tight hug. Man, just like old times, her crib smelled like heaven because she always started cooking dinner early. I rubbed my hands together and licked my lips. I planned on packing some food up but I needed to holla at this nigga Teddy first. I assumed when he got out he'd go to his mother's to recover but nah, this nigga was in some apartment I didn't even know he had.

My aunt swatted my shoulder and replied, "Alright now, greedy ass. I missed you. Gon' on now, I'll make you some plates."

"I missed you too, auntie. How's Teddy holding up since being out the hospital?" I folded my arms across my chest.

My aunt tightened her lips and shook her head. "I'm just gonna say a prayer that this won't be the last year I see my son alive because the way that boy is so silent just means he's thinking dangerous thoughts. I haven't seen him and he ain't answering my calls. Maybe you can talk to him for me, Syncere. You've always been the more level-headed one outta y'alls crazy asses."

I rubbed my chin in deep thought. I had a feeling I knew where Teddy's mind was at because if niggas tried to take my life, my mind would be on the same shit. I would be trying to find the muthafuckas responsible and my cousin was on the same shit. But, to pacify my aunt, I told her I'd talk to him and see what was up. We had other shit to discuss anyway.

"Aight, lemme go holla at him." I kissed her cheek and grabbed the foil plates of food she packed up for me. Leaving out of her house, I left to go scoop Teddy. When I got to his new spot, I was surprised at how he was holding up. It was amazing what prayer, money and some surgery could do. Hopping in my whip, he dapped me up. "Welcome back, cuh." I said.

"Good looks, nigga. Yo', why this nigga Heem ain't come check me in the hospital, cuh? Why this nigga been ducking my calls since last night? Huh?"

"Nigga, I don't know. I ain't that man's keeper." I told him, driving with the flow of traffic. Sparking up some weed, I continued, "As far as him not coming up there at all, yeah, that's fucked up. Y'all been bros for a grip, right? I know that money be calling though so I don't know." I shrugged my shoulders.

"Nigga, fuck the money!" Teddy yelled and pounded his fist into his other open hand. "I know that nigga set me up and I wanna know why before I kill his ass. Straight like that! Might even shoot his bitch too." His nostrils flared as he glared at me.

I looked over at this nigga like he was crazy and questioned, "What? Have you lost yo' mind?"

"Have you? Since when you so trusting of a muthafucka?! I've known that nigga longer than you and when I'm telling you some shit ain't smelling right, hear what the fuck I'm saying, cuh!" He aggressively pointed to his ear.

"Teddy, I'm hearing you. Calm the fuck down and talk to me without all this yelling bullshit."

Teddy rubbed his shoulder blade and sighed heavily before he spoke. Then, he said, "This ain't the first time I done been shot at, cuh." He raised his shirt to reveal an ugly ass scar on the right side of his rib cage and another small one over his chest. Shaking his head, "This nigga Heem was right there making sure a nigga stayed alive and when it was time to ride out on the pussy niggas who got me, there wasn't even a need for a fucking conversation, feel me?"

He put his shirt down and twisted his mouth up. "This time was different. Syncere, I almost died in that fucking ambulance! And all I get is a few messages through you?" Teddy was hot. Shaking his head again, he just stared out the window. "Nah, cuh. My soul telling me something's foul. I mean, I know I been dabbing more with the coke and shit and my money been a little funny but I always correct that shit. Ain't no reason to be calling hits out on a supposed brother of his." He glanced in my direction. I rubbed my chin as I took in all of his words and tried to process all of what he was saying to me.

"And you saying last time the nigga was right there?"

"Every step of the way and shot that nigga in the back of his neck for me. No conversation needed. What makes this time so different?" Teddy asked me.

I was thinking his ass was a little paranoid and overthinking shit. Faheem and him were close as fuck but if he felt this strongly about this situation, I was going to make it my duty to find some shit out. "Aight, so what you wanna do? You could set up a meeting with that nigga and do shit the *right way*." I put emphasis on 'the right way'. I knew this nigga was already seeing bloodshed.

"Fuck that talking shit, cuh. I know I'm right and all I need is the right space and opportunity to handle this shit."

"Nigga, them hospital drugs got you talking crazy. I'll see what's with it though."

"That nigga ain't shit, Syncere. I'm starting to see that and the sooner you realize that, the sooner you gon' be on my wave. Go 'head and talk to that nigga if you want to but just know he got something coming his way." I nodded my head and the car grew silent as we smoked and made our rounds. After a few, I dropped Teddy back off to his whip and told him to get his mind right while I figured some shit out too.

Driving away, I felt conflicted as a muthafucka. I checked my phone and I noticed I had a text from Faheem asking me to come pick up a package at his crib. There was another text from P asking what I was up to. I hit Faheem back asking for the address then looked at her text again. I started not to respond to it but my feelings wouldn't let me. It bothered me that we could go days without speaking yet she was always on my mind. I'd hit her up and get no response. I would call and get no call back. P even ignored my Facetime calls. I definitely wasn't the type to chase a bitch but she was far from a bitch. She was a Queen who didn't even know it. I was really feeling P and wanted to show her all that she was worth.

I hated that she had a whole nigga who didn't even appreciate her ass yet she still was with him. There was only so much temptation a nigga could take. Knowing P wasn't happy had me questioning why she was staying in a relationship she wasn't benefiting from. I could tell ol' boy supplied her with the finer things in life but shorty could hold her own. There wasn't that much love in be world to stay where you're not wanted. For now though, I was playing my position, whatever that was. When the time was right, she'd be mine regardless. I hit this nigga O telling him I was on the way and then texted P back:

*ME: I'm coolin'. What it do?*

*P: Oh, I'm just at one of my stores going over these sales reports. I'm trying to figure out the next steps for this fourth store.*

*ME: Oh, ok then. Get to work.*

*P: Yeah, it's kind of slow today. Got a lot on my mind too. Ugh...*

*ME: Damn.*

*P: Lol yeah... I miss you like crazy though. I can't believe you got me feeling like this.*

I looked at that text and shook my head. I didn't get the feeling she was bullshitting me but if she was tired enough of dealing with that nigga, she'd be showing me she missed me. Fuck the words, I was believed in actions. I hit her with the simplest reply I could think of.

*ME: That's what's up.*

*P: Yeah, I wanna see you.*

*ME: Oh yeah. For what?*

*P: Umm, are you okay? I'm feeling a little disconnect here. You don't miss me?*

*ME: I wouldn't have to miss you if you would stop fucking around and really come fuck with a real one. You must enjoy being mistreated, huh? The dick that good or are the gifts that special?*

I knew I was going to strike a nerve with that last text, but truth be told, I didn't give a fuck. I was tired of the cat and mouse conversation. I had better shit to do. P FaceTimed me and I rejected the call. Once more she tried and I did the same shit. A text from her came through that read:

*P: Look, idk what your problem is! You knew I had a nigga from jump and while shits not perfect I know he loves me. I'm just conflicted with my feelings right now since I met you. No bullshit, this shit is crazy.*

*ME: Don't let shit get too crazy. Do ya thang, P. It's obvious where yo' heart is at. Stop fucking with mine.*

*P: So, what you saying, Syncere? You leaving me hanging?*

*ME: I always give people enough rope to hang themselves. When you ready to walk away from something that no longer brings you a peace of mind, you'll cut the rope. 'Til then, I'm good, love. Enjoy."*

She called me three times back to back to back and I rejected every single call before telling her I'd talk to her some other time. I put my phone on DND and continued the drive to Faheem's crib. Blocking P from my mind, I bumped some trap music. Fuck it, I wasn't putting myself out there with her ass no more. *It is what the fuck it is*, I told myself.

\*\*\*

I parked my Nav outside this nigga's crib and just stared at the house. Faheem and his bitch was living like a fucking King and Queen with their big ass spot out in the boonies. My lil' two-story crib didn't compare but it was nothing a little more money and time couldn't get me. I hopped out of my whip and called this nigga as I walked to the door.

"What up, cuh?" Saige opened the door all cheesy.

"Shit, man. Cooling, you know." I stepped inside and asked, "Where this nigga Heem at? He told me to meet him here."

"Yeah, we downstairs."

I took a brief look around and admired the layout of the crib. I followed Saige down to this game room where Faheem was smoking a blunt flicking through the channels on the plasma. A bottle of some 1738 and a few dismantled guns sat on the glass table his feet were up on. My thoughts circled to the shit Teddy was spitting and I quickly pushed that thought to the back of my mind for a minute.

"What up, cuh? What it do?" He greeted me with a head nod without looking in my direction.

Saige plopped down on the couch beside his brother with his arms folded across his chest. They both looked up at me and he laughed. "You not gon' sit nigga?"

I glanced back and forth between the both of them and replied, "I just came for a package, right? I kinda got some shit to take care of," I lied. I wasn't feeling the vibe and I was heated that I left my gun in the glove compartment in the whip. Teddy's ass had me paranoid around these niggas right now.

Faheem turned the TV off and planted his feet on the carpet. Sitting forward, he said, "I got the package but I got some shit to holla at you about first."

"Oh yeah, what's that?"

"My connect wants to triple the work he giving me and with Teddy still in the hospital and shit, I need to know if you that nigga to take on more product. Can you handle it?"

"Oh, you ain't know that nigga's outta the hospital?"

Faheem raised his eyebrow, clearly shocked to hear that part. See, I didn't tell him the day that Teddy would be released. I wanted to see if he gave a fuck enough to ask about him. Judging from the assumptions my cousin made and the way Faheem was being funny about letting Teddy back in the business struck me as odd. There was definitely was something up.

"Oh for real? You ain't mention that to me."

"You didn't ask, did you?" I challenged Faheem and we locked eyes. Saige stood up and looked back and forth between us.

Laughing, he jumped in and asked, "What, y'all niggas 'bouta fight or something? What the fuck is the issue right now? If that nigga Teddy ready to bounce back, then it's nothing at all to get this work off."

I was starting to think Saige was a little slow and couldn't pick up on energy or certain shit his brother did regardless of how close they were. Man, anybody could feel the tension in the room. That shit was thicker than a bitch.

Faheem said, "We good." He continued to smoke then glared in my direction. Eyeballing me, he said, "We 'bouta take this flight to Philly for the weekend. You down, cuh?"

Glancing over at Saige as he sat back down on the couch, I had a weird feeling about all this shit but I kept my cool for now. I had a feeling I wouldn't make it back to Carol City if I took that flight. I wasn't feeling neither one of these muthafuckas vibes at all. Looking back towards Faheem, I shook my head and responded, "Nah, I got some shit to handle. I'll be ready to distribute that work when you get back though."

He nodded his head behind me towards the couch then said, "Don't forget to take that behind you." I walked over to pick up a tiny black Gucci book bag. I unzipped it and there were a couple stacks of money inside. "What's this?" I asked him.

Faheem smirked at me and replied, "For that nigga, Teddy. He's always good on this side, cuh. Nice to have him back. I'll be in touch with y'all when we get back. Tell that nigga stay up." Just like that, he turned his attention back to the TV.

I scoffed and pinched the bridge of my nose. I took the bag and proceeded to walk out of the room. I heard Faheem ask Saige something about some stripper hoes. For a nigga with a whole bitch at home, he wasn't shit when it came to being faithful to her. She definitely deserved a new nigga. Faheem tossing me money form Teddy had me a little confused about shit. Nonetheless, something was off, and everything would get addressed when them niggas got back to Miami.

# CHAPTER NINE

# PEYTON

"Fuck it, P. Fuck him!"

I hung up the phone after trying to call Syncere for the fifth time. My calls were going straight to voicemail and I was fuming mad. This nigga had me hot! Who the fuck did he think he was telling me that I must like being mistreated? He didn't know shit except for what I told him. If Syncere wanted to act like this, I didn't need to be fucking with him.

I sadly shook my head. I wasn't no better than Faheem to even have started fucking with Syncere to begin with. I had to leave it alone even though every fiber of my being was telling me to give him a shot regardless of a ring another nigga gave me. I picked up my phone to call Faheem since I hadn't heard from him all damn day and it was going on three in the afternoon. Just as I was about to click on his name to make the call, I heard giggles from inside the store.

"Yeah and this uppity bitch swear she's the only one bouncing on that big dick! Girl bye, all of Miami done tasted Faheem's dick, including me, okayyy!"

I recognized the voice as Diamond's and immediately got hot all over again. I know this bitch didn't just say she fucked with my fiancé! Really though?! Walking over to my closed office door, I heard her heels click clacking towards my office. I swung the door open and watched the color drain from her already pale ass face. She ended her call with the quickness.

"P-Peyton, I...I didn't know you was in here, girl."

I didn't even say shit back to her. Instead, I slapped the shit out of the bitch and her cell phone flew out of her hand. "What was that shit you was just talking about?" I snatched my big ass hoops out of my ears and rolled up my sleeves. "Bitch, I *know* I didn't just hear you say you been fucking Faheem."

Diamond held her cheek and glared at me. She said, "If you wanna know the truth, damn near all of Miami done fucked your man, sis. The way that nigga slangs that dick, I'm surprised your pussy hasn't fallen off," she smirked at me.

I charged at this bitch and uppercut her in the stomach. I watched as Diamond coughed up a lung and held her belly. "You lil' hoe ass bitch!" I yelled. I tried grabbing her neck and she spit in my face.

"Bitch, fuck you!" Diamond barked, still holding her stomach. "I don't owe you no loyalty, yo' so-called nigga does!"

I swung at the bitch with a hanger and she took off running behind the register looking for something to hit me with I assumed. Wiping my face off, I walked over to lock the door to the store then turned around to face her with my heart pounding. I hollered, "Bitch, I trusted you! You gon' catch this fucking beat down and then I'mma check this nigga." I ran behind the counter and Diamond tossed the wireless keyboard at me. I ducked and laughed because it was then I realized this bitch couldn't fight worth shit. Oh yeah, she was catching this ass whooping! "Bitch!" I smacked her twice in the face with the wire hanger and grabbed a handful of her hair, pulling her downwards.

"Let me fucking go!" Diamond shouted as she tried to free herself from my hold. Punching the back of her head, I kneed her in the face and then punched her in the nose. This time, I drew blood. She was barely able to stand up straight.

"Bitch, I had you in my fucking place of business just to find out you was in my man's face!"

With her face covered in welts and her nose leaking, she spit up blood and yelled, "And all on his dick too!"

I couldn't believe she was still talking shit. I kicked the bitch in the stomach and she flew onto the floor. Standing over her, I watched as she curled up in a ball and cried. "Get up," I told her.

"I'm done with you. Get the fuck up outta my store!"

"I can't get up right now!" Diamond cried out.

Reaching for the store phone, I picked it up. "That ain't my problem, *sis*! Either you get the fuck out on your own or I can have somebody come clean your ass up. You know I got clout around this bitch." Glancing up at me, Diamond saw I was serious and slowly started to move. "You ain't moving fast enough. Get the fuck out!" I picked up the wire hanger again.

She scrambled to her feet and went to grab her cell phone from the floor. "He's still gon' fuck around, Peyton. Yo' nigga is a certified hoe!" Diamond unlocked the store door and added, "Just tell that nigga I still want my fucking money for the baby he made me abort!" Running towards the door, she hauled ass out of the store and down the street. Some bystanders on the strip were started peeking into the store.

"What the fuck are you looking at?! You want a piece too?!" I barked at then. Rolling my eyes, I shut the door and stormed off into my office. I was too fucking through. I grabbed my shit and locked the store for the day. I'd have to deal with the mess another time. Once in my truck, I called Milah and I could tell she rejected my call so I called again and she did the same thing. I broke down. First Syncere was brushing me off and then this fuck shit with Faheem's disrespectful ass once again. I was feeling so sick to know that even Diamond had carried my fiancé's seed and to make matters worse, I didn't have my best friend to vent. My sister and mother was off limits at this point. A bitch felt lonely as hell. I banged my head against the steering wheel and let out a frustrated scream.

"Daddy, I need you!" I sobbed. "I fucking need you. Why did you have to leave me?! Whyyyyyy?" My phone rang and surprisingly, it was Faheem. Wiping my tears, I immediately picked up. "Where the fuck are you at?"

"Damn baby, what's the matter?"

"Don't fucking *baby* me, Faheem? Where the fuck are you?"

"I just picked up Saraj from daycare. Fuck you sounding all fucking crazy for?"

"Meet me at the fucking house *now*!" I ended the call, started up the truck and zoomed off in traffic. "This nigga done played with me for the last fucking time! I promise you that!" I spoke aloud to myself.

***

Pulling up to the house, I noticed his car was in the driveway. I swear, I was about to catch a body and I didn't give a fuck. I was tired of this shit. No matter how many chances I gave and how many times Faheem said he would do better it never happened. Enough was enough. I grabbed my purse and jumped out of my Rover.

Opening the door, I yelled, "Faheem!" I slammed the door and tossed the keys on the coffee table. I climbed the staircase taking two steps at a time to get to his ass, yelling the whole way. "Heem, where the fuck are you?!"

"I just laid Saraj down for a nap in her room. What the fuck is the problem, Peyton?" He asked, obviously annoyed. As soon as I reached the bedroom, this nigga was fresh out of the shower with a towel wrapped around his waist. I hauled off and slapped the shit out of him.

"I'm sick of your shit!" I proceeded to pound on his chest. The fact that Saraj was sleeping feet away down the hall didn't faze me whatsoever.

"What the fuck is yo' problem?!" He shouted and held my wrists.

"Nigga, you're my fucking problem! You really don't know how to keep your dick in ya pants?! Is it really that fucking hard?" I struggled to get my fists loose and opted to kick him in the nuts instead. Kneeling over in discomfort, Faheem groaned.

"What the fuck are you talking about? I ain't

been doing shit!"

"Oh, so you ain't fucking Diamond? The lil' bitch said she was pregnant before too! Really, my nigga?" I huffed and puffed as I folded my arms across my chest. Looking him up and down, I felt disgusted being in his presence. "Go ahead and lie so I can slap the fuck outta you again!" The look on his face was telling me it was true and I started to cry all over again.

Coming towards me, he replied, "I can explain that though."

Slapping his ass again, I said, "I don't wanna hear it! Fuck you! Fuck this relationship! I'm done!"

"You're done? You must be crazy. You ain't done with shit!"

"Fuck you!" I snatched my ring off and tossed it at him before turning to leave. Faheem pulled me back and slapped me onto the bed.

"I suggest you calm the fuck down and keep yo' fucking hands to yo'self. I done told you about that shit, P." He spoke hastily as he climbed on top of me. I spit in his face just as his hoe Diamond had done to me and repeated myself.

"Fuck you!"

He glared at me and shouted, "Man, you really done lost yo' fucking mind!" He wiped the spit off his face and said, "Yes, I fucked with Diamond in the past and she agreed to get the abortion. The bitch been blackmailing me outta some dough ever since just so she wouldn't tell you shit. That's the truth for yo' ass! You happy now?" Faheem hopped off the bed and started pacing the floor, looking like he me wanted to kill me.

I just sat there crying and shaking my head. What the fuck was wrong with me that this nigga couldn't be satisfied with just *me*? "Why can't you just be with me and only me? Why don't you love me?" I cried aloud.

"I do love you, P." He spoke calmly. "I just have a bad habit of fucking other bitches from time to time. It ain't 'bout nothing though." I sat up and stared at him with tears streaming down my face. We locked eyes as he continued, "We can go pick you out another ring before I hop on this flight to Philly this weekend."

I scoffed. "You're stupid, you know that? I'm done, Heem." I climbed off the bed and he grabbed my wrist.

"You really tryna leave a nigga right now?" My whole body tensed up when he started caressing my cheek, he said, "I can't let another nigga see how great of a woman you are. You know I love you."

"No, you don't."

Cupping my face, he forced a kiss on me. "I do love you. I'm sorry for all this dumb shit." He slapped my ass and strolled into the walk-in closet stark naked, probably feeling like a king. Faheem was becoming worse and worse and I feared that nigga would really try to hurt me. Fuck what he was saying, I was done.

# FAHEEM

"What's good, son? I'm sorry daddy hasn't been around like that lately. I just been working so much. You know, so I can get you them nice ass J's you like so much. You know how you stunt on 'em in school." I laughed into the phone but I could tell Junior wasn't fucking with me. This was yet time I had dissed him and like the bitch his mama was, Whitney called me up. Instead of leaving him hanging like I'd been doing, she wanted me to tell him why I wasn't coming to get him. What could I really say though? I just had to take care of business.

"Mm-hmm, you can't put the streets on hold for a few hours for yo' fucking son, but I bet you if that bitch Faye needed you, ya punk ass would go running to her!" Whitney shouted in the background. "You ain't shit nigga! Junior, hang up the goddamn phone!"

"Bitch-" I had to stop myself from going off being that my son was the actual one on the phone. "My bad, jit."

"It's cool," Junior sighed. "I get it, pops. I'm not a baby anymore." He told me. "I miss hanging out with you though. Take it easy." And just like that, the call ended.

"Fuck, cuh!" I lashed out, tossing my phone at the wall. First, I go to pick up Sayona to take her ass to the abortion clinic and this bitch's number was disconnected. I just knew she was trying to pull a fast one on me and that shit had me hotter than a bitch. Then, I get a call from my Philly connect about tripling my supply. I was already doing the damn thing out here so this just meant more money, power and respect. I needed all my niggas on the same page so I told Syncere to swing through. Even though I was still plotting on this nigga Teddy, I still needed my fucking work moved and my money made. I could tell Syncere was feeling some type of way about some shit but I didn't let that affect what I was trying to do. He was either gon' stay down or get laid the fuck down.

Next, I get a call from Saraj's daycare saying she was flipping out crying and having a bad temper tantrum. They come talking about they couldn't get a hold of Faye's ass so I had to drop what I was doing midday to go pick my daughter up. By the time Peyton called me up screaming and bitching, man, my fucking head was booming so badly.

I snapped when she mentioned finally leaving me. After the day I had plus the weird dream not too long ago, she had me fucked up! I'd be damned if someone else got her. All bullshit aside, I did love her ass. I figured I'd buy her bigger ring and officially set a date to get married so she'd shut her ass up. After demanding that she suck my dick, I fucked P into a deep sleep and got ready to leave the crib later that night. I kissed her forehead whispered, "I love you."

*RING! RING! RING! RING!*

I silenced my phone to be sure not to awake Peyton and noticed it was my brother hitting me up. I was on my way out the door to go see what was good with this bitch Sayona for the second time today and I wasn't trying to be distracted. Ignoring his call, I continued to head to her crib. I pulled in the raggedy housing complex and hopped out of my truck. It was almost ten at night and her ass was big as hell carrying them fucking twins. I figured she was home by now thinking she was gon' get away with ducking me. If she wasn't, whoever she stayed with her knew something about her whereabouts. I pounded on the front door and waited for someone to answer.

"Yeah, who it is out there?" The screen door flew open and there stood a nappy-headed, scrawny, ashy lip, saggy titty looking crack head. She hugged her robe close to her body and kissed her teeth. "Mmmm, may I help yo' fine ass?"

I paused for a moment and continued to look her up and down. "Yeah, I'm looking for Sayona She here?"

Stepping aside, the lady gave me a view of the trashed living room and replied, "Do it look like she home? Shit, you interrupting my shows now. Damn." The lady started to close the screen door and I put my foot against it. Taking a look around the deserted housing complex, I pulled two nice size bumps out of my boxers and held them out to her. I died laughing on the inside as I watched her eyes grow wide and she licked her lips.

"Uh huh, you like that? That's what you want?" As she went to reach for them, I snatched them back. "Tell me where the fuck Sayona at."

She started rubbing her hands together as she leaned against the door frame. "Man, I swear for God, I don't know. She left up outta here with some lil' ugly muthafucka in a yellow car."

I stepped a little closer to her and squinted my eyes. "How long did they leave? What kinda car did they drive off in?"

"I don't know what kind. I just said it was yellow, goddamn!" The lady told me as she cut her eyes at me. "Between you and me, I can't stand that lil' bitch though. Hmph, I never have! I don't know why I had the fucka." She did a little dance with her middle fingers in the air. "That's for her! Now, can I get them beauties in yo' hand, mister sir?" She flashed a wide grin at me, and I almost threw up. Damn near all of her teeth were missing.

I grilled the fuck out of this fiend bitch before me and handed her the two rocks. "Good looks on the info."

She quickly shoved the rocks in her dingy panties and winked at me. "No, thank you." She stated then wiped her nose and leaned closer to me. "Lemme put these gums on you and get another one. How 'bout it?"

I stepped back away from her nasty looking ass watching her lick her lips. Disgusted didn't even describe how I felt. I loved getting my dick sucked more than the average nigga, but her ass probably had some incurable shit. I was all the way set. She served her purpose.

"Man, you better be happy with what you got. If you hear from either one of them bitches, you never saw me." Lifting up my hoodie, I flashed the handle on my gun.

"Okay, alright. Mm-hmm. Mr. Fine ass with the big rock jawns. You got it." She snapped her fingers and went back in the crib.

Jumping in my whip, I screeched out of the complex happier than a bitch. Sayona probably knew them fucking babies weren't mine and her ass ran off with the twins' father. Or maybe she ran off with some other nigga. Either way, she was that man's problem now. I had more important shit to handle.

Before hopping on this flight to Philly in two days, there was some unfinished business to tend to Teddy still being one of them. I knew once he was told about the product extension, shit would quickly go back to normal and I'd have the opportunity to catch him lacking again. My phone alerted me of a text message and it was from a random number. The shit read:

*You ain't the king of shit out here. Yo' days are numbered. Count 'em.*

I sat there in the middle of the road with cars honking their horns at me. Looking around at people walking the streets, I wanted to know who the fuck was really out here threatening me. I had too much shit going on.

# CHAPTER TEN

# SYNCERE

*"When I say to the wicked, 'You wicked person, you will surely die,' and you do not speak out to dissuade them from their ways, that wicked person will die for their sin, and I will hold you accountable for their blood. But if you do warn the wicked person to turn from their ways and they do not do so, they will die for their sin, though you yourself will be saved."*

"Amen."

As I sat on the edge of my bed finishing the prayer, I opened my eyes and took a look behind me. P was staring back looking so fucking beautiful yet stressed out. It blew my mind to know her nigga was really doing her dirty. I had just left the liquor store and was on my way to the crib for the night when she called me crying her ass off, saying she'd got into a heated ass argument with the nigga. It took everything in me not to come get her and blow his head off. Instead, she asked for my address and in no time at all, she was at my doorstep with a duffle bag packed and a tear stained face.

"I can't do this anymore, Syncere," P told me, wrapping her arounds around my waist. Resting her chin against me, she said, "I really feel like shit's gon' get crazy 'cause he knows I'm really fed he fuck up."

Holding her in my arms, I replied, "Everything gon' be straight. I'mma deal with that nigga. I need some info on his ass."

"No!" She quickly objected. "I don't want you doing anything crazy 'cause..."

"Crazy? We past that part. I fucks with you heavy, P!" I exploded. "You run to me with a packed bag and a snotty ass nose and expect me to let this shit slide? Nah, cuh, you got me fucked up. Like I said, I'mma holla at the nigga and whatever happens, fucking happens."

P climbed off my bed and started putting her clothes on. "Maybe I shoulda never came here."

Stopping her from leaving, I said, "Maybe you shouldn't have but you did, so now what? You gon' run from here and run right back to the muthafucka?"

"Yo', you just don't get it..." she chuckled and shook her head as she looked down at her shoes.

"I don't! Explain the shit to me, P. You fucking with a nigga who clearly don't mean you no good and you fighting the shit! You battling with yo' mind and yo' heart. What the fuck do you want?" I asked angrily because truth be told, I was tired of her back and forth bullshit at this point. "Tell me what the fuck you wanna do and we can do that shit."

P bit her bottom lip and stared up at me in silence. I stared back, trying to read her fucking mind. After a few moments, she finally spoke up. "I just wanna be happy, Syncere. I deserve it."

I pinched the bridge of my nose and let out a frustrated sigh. Taking her hand, I sat on the bed and placed her on my lap. "Listen, P. Happiness is a state of mind and it starts from within. I've only known you for a hot second, but you got a lot going for yo' self and you're beautiful. I can tell you gotta big ass heart. You gotta do what make you happy. Fuck tryna please a nigga who ain't even appreciating yo' worth 'cause it's gon' diminish yo' shine. Understand what I'm saying to you?" I asked her. "I'm growing to care for you and I'll lay that nigga out for you in a second. All you gotta do is say the fucking word. Let a nigga know you really moving the fuck on for good, P. What's up?"

I laid everything on the table and let the dice roll, something I never did. P swallowed hard and I watched the tears fall from her brown eyes. She nodded her head as if she was agreeing to what I said. "I hear you, I do." She told me.

"Aight. So, what's it gon' be? You either with him or you with me. And if you with me, I'mma see to it that the nigga ain't disrespecting you no more and that's on me."

P laid her head against my chest and sighed heavily. Looking up at me, she kissed my lips and said, "I'm with you."

I kissed her back, happy as shit on the inside. My phone vibrating. It was Teddy hitting me up and I immediately answered the call. It was hella late and I just knew something was wrong. "Hold on, P. What it do, cuh?" I left out of the room and went into the kitchen. Opening the fridge, I pulled out the Remy bottle and chugged it. It was that type of morning. Only thing on my mind was killing a bitch nigga.

"Where you at?"

"Nigga, where else would I be? What you on?" I questioned, skeptically. "You good?"

"Nah, nigga. My mind racing. I been up getting blazed tryna find this bitch Milah, man.."

I sucked my teeth. "Milah? Why, what's good?"

"Yeah nigga, I been throwing some money in this lil' safe for a couple months now and a lil' piece of jewelry. Man, I must've left the shit open or this bitch sneaky as fuck, cuh! I give her ass whatever she asks for, so why would she take my shit? I'm hot, nigga!" Teddy hollered. "There was like two hundred bands in that fucking safe!"

Shaking my head, I told him, "First off, stop all this fucking yelling. Secondly, yo' first fuck up was fucking with that bitch to begin with. I knew I didn't like her ass for a reason." Teddy tried cutting me off but I said, "Nah nigga, hear me out. You probably don't even trust Milah like that anyway. She been seemed like a lil' money hungry hippo ass hoe. As soon as you get out the hospital, I bet she was right there, all smiles, huh?"

"That fucking bitch, cuh. I'mma find her ass and put a fucking bullet in her skull. That's all I know! This shit real personal."

"I feel you," I replied and took a seat at the table. Rubbing my chin, I got back to the conversation. "The question is, where did she go? Everybody know everybody in Carol City, nigga. She shouldn't be that hard to track down."

"I'mma get her ass, cuh. I told Saige to keep a look out for her ass too" This nigga was about to start a war and a search team over this Milah bitch. I laughed and Teddy said, "Yeah aight, keep laughing, Syncere. I'mma get him, Milah and Heem all together and merk every last one of them muthafuckas. I know Saige gotta know his brother set that hit up." He was talking so crazy but I knew my cousin was a joking ass nigga so I couldn't tell how serious he was.

Looking over my shoulder to see if P was coming, I said, "You sound real serious about all this shit, cuh. Yo' ass gon' murk the nigga based off an assumption and a hunch. Plus, I forgot to mention this nigga was holding some dough for you too and-"

"Fuck that bread and fuck that nigga! Straight up, on everything, I know I'm right. Either you riding with me or you not, cuh. I don't even give a fuck!"

"Aight, hold on. I gotta take care of some shit tomorrow then I'mma get with you."

"Fuck that! Meet me at this nigga Heem's crib. I'mma text you the address." *CLICK!*

"Shit!"

"Everything alright?" I turned around and P was standing in the doorway looking all innocent and cute. I approached her and kissed her lips as I palmed her ass.

"It will be. You good?"

"Yeah, I'm good with you."

"I told you." Kissing her again, I said, "I gotta go with my cousin to handle some shit but I'll be back, aight?"

"I don't wanna be alone right now, Syncere." P wrapped her arms around my neck and asked, "Can I ride with you and we can talk some more?"

"I'm with that but first," I picked her up and

217

she giggled as she wrapped her legs around my waist. "I need to taste that pussy."

Laughing back, she said, "Boy, you crazy."

# PEYTON

I was feeling some type of way about calling up Syncere. Faheem's ass thought he left me sound asleep when in reality, I was plotting. No sooner than I heard his car start up, I kicked the covers back and hopped up out of the bed. I'd made up my mind that I was leaving for good and threw on some sweatpants, a T-Shirt and some kicks. I tossed some clothes and jewelry along with a few stacks of money I had laying around the crib into one of my large purses. I didn't care about Milah pulling a funny ass disappearing act. I didn't care about Faheem. I didn't care about Saraj sleeping upstairs. I didn't care about shit except leaving. As I drove to Syncere's crib, I was on some fuck every-body type of shit.

As Syncere ate my pussy like it was a bomb ass buffet dinner, my thoughts wandered to what the hell Faheem could be thinking or doing. I just knew he was calling my phone and sending texts but for the final time, I blocked his ass. Syncere and I got dressed and left his house hand in hand, heading to meet this cousin of his. On the way, we listened to some throwback Biggie and de-bated about who was the greatest between him or Tupac. He had me cracking up and it felt good to laugh after all the crying I'd been doing lately. After like twenty minutes of debating, I cut the music off and blurted out, "So are you gonna hurt him?"

Cutting his eyes at me, Syncere responded, "Don't even ask me no shit like that. I said what I said. He gon' be dealt with and he ain't gon' be disrespecting you no more. That's it, P." He cranked the music back up and I sat back.

Pouting like a lil' baby, I looked over at him. I didn't want to drop the subject but it kept gnawing at me. I just had to know what we were about to get ourselves into. I was feeling Syncere and loved the way he made me feel inside. The thought of starting over with him really did sound good but I just knew Faheem wouldn't take that L lying down. Reaching over to turn the music back down, I stated, "I believe in karma. Good karma and bad karma. Let's just leave Miami together and never look back. Fuck him, Syncere."

"I can't do that, P. I don't run from shit. Why the fuck you worried about what happens to this nigga? Here you go again, battling yo'self."

"I just don't want that shit on my conscience!" I told him. "I'm not battling shit. Stop saying that. Clearly, I done made my fucking decision." He glanced over in my direction and I rolled my eyes before looking out the window. His phone rang just as he was about to respond to what

I said.

"Yeah nigga, I'm on my way there. I ain't 'bouta let you do some wild shit by yo' self. I'm telling you, talk with that nigga and see where his mind at, cuh. Aight, man, I'll be pulling up soon." He ended the call and gripped the steering wheel looking frustrated.

"Where we going again? What's your cousin's name?" I asked with my eyebrow raised as I peeped we were passing this store not too far from me and Faheem's crib.

"I doubt you know my wild ass cousin Teddy. You don't seem too into these streets, Pretty P." Taking my hand into his, Syncere told me, "You be about yo' business and shit. That's what I love about you."

Instantly, I felt panic in my chest and my breathing became labored. "T-Teddy? With the dreads?" I glanced over at him, praying his said hell nah but instead, I heard the opposite.

"Yeah, that's my cousin. How you know this nigga?"

I watched as we slowly pulled up in front of my crib and the first thing I noticed was Faheem's car parked in the driveway. My palms began to moisten so I rubbed them and closed my eyes really praying this was a big ass dream. "Lord, please don't let this be happening right now. Please." Syncere threw his truck in park and gripped my thigh.

"P, talk to me. How you know my cousin?"

"Syncere, why are we meeting your cousin here?"

"I asked you a question first." He eyeballed the shit out of me and squinted his eyes. "What's good?"

"There's something I gotta tell you."

"Well, spit that shit out then!"

"Alright, alright! Look, I live here with my fiancé. His name's Faheem and I know Teddy because he's been in his crew for years. They run these streets."

"Faheem? That's the nigga you been dealing with? That's the nigga who's been fucking around on you? That's the nigga who's been mistreating yo' heart? Faheem?" Syncere questioned, searching my eyes for some type of signal of a lie, I assume.

I nodded my head and replied, "Yes. How do you know him?"

"You told me yo' name was P..."

"No, I told you that you can *call* me P." I quickly reminded him and turned his face towards mine. "It's Peyton."

Syncere dropped his head and mumbled, "This muthafucka even got yo' name tatted." He shook his head and looked over at me.

"Yeah, on his neck. His baby's mother even tried to be funny and get a tatt on...nevermind, I-"

"How the fuck did I miss this shit?"

Tires came screeching around the corner and sure enough, Teddy hopped out of his Lambo and walked over to the Navigator we sat in. He banged on the driver's side window and Syncere looked over at me before rolling it down.

"What's good, nig... Peyton? What the fuck you doing with my cousin?"

"What *you* doing here, Teddy? Somebody, please tell me what the fuck is up."

"We been kicking it."

"Oh shit, you been fucking around on this nigga Heem?" Teddy asked me, leaning all into the window and shit.

"Teddy, bye! You done been around Faheem's ol' trifling community dick having ass when he's fucked other bitches. I'm almost sure of it. Now, one of y'all better explain to me why we're here right now!" My head was spinning and, in another minute or so, I was going to make a run for it and leave both of them standing outside.

Teddy cocked his gun back and said, "It's

nothing person towards you, P, but I got a bone to pick with yo' fiancé."

"Yeah, well this shit just got personal for me. Watch out." Syncere spoke coldly as he opened the door to hop out.

"What? Wait a minute, y'all…" I quickly exited his Nav and grabbed hold of his arm as we all walked up the driveway.

"P, you tripping. Niggas ain't waiting for shit. My cousin feeling a way about this nigga and now that I know it was him the whole time hurting yo' ass, fucks no. He gotta go." Syncere yanked way from me and pushed me towards the door. "Go knock on the door." He told me and I hesitated, feeling my whole body began to tremble.

"Peyton, knock on the fucking door please or I'mma just start shooting through the windows and wake everybody the fuck up." Teddy grilled the fuck out of me.

"This is for yo' protection. You wanna be happy, right?" Syncere asked me. "So, do what you gotta do."

I sniffled then moved closer to the door. I thought to myself, how the fuck was the world really this small? Faheem kept his business to himself so I would have never known about Syncere being down with his crew. For as long as I could remember, his main niggas were Saige and

Teddy. Instead of knocking on my front door, I rang the doorbell then peered over my shoulder at these niggas. We all stared back at each other.

I remembered the day I met Syncere. He did just pop up out of nowhere hitting my car and then again, that night on the bridge. He was too caring and nice to me from jump. Was this all a set up? Was this even really happening right now? Was Faheem gon' open this door and kill me on sight for cheating on him? Was...

The door swung open and there he stood. I froze up. Faheem's gaze was deadly from his bloodshot eyes. He flexed his jaw and sucked his teeth then lunged for me. Grabbing hold of my neck, this nigga dragged me inside the crib.

"Peyton, are you fucking crazy?" He asked, cracking his neck. He walked over to the front door to kick it close when Syncere appeared in the doorway with his gun raised and Teddy behind him, ready to bust his gun as well. "Fuck y'all niggas doing?" Faheem asked, backing up a little bit.

"You got me fucked up right now, cuh," Syncere stated aggressively.

Teddy rushed in from behind and pushed him aside. Kicking the door closed, he hollered, "Fuck all his talking! I'mma ask you one question and that's it." All I needed was for one of these niggas guns to go off and hit my ass. It was about to go down.

Faheem glared at all of us and asked, "Aye, what the fuck y'all niggas on?"

"Did you or did you not send them niggas to kill me?" Teddy questioned him back.

"Fuck you talking 'bout nigga? Get the fuck outta here with this shit." He brushed him off and looked over at me. "I need to deal with this bitch right now."

"P, come here," Syncere told me. I ran to his side and he held my shaky hand. "You done lost a real one, cuh? It's over for you."

"What, you been fucking my bitch, nigga?"

"Yup, he been digging all up in that pussy!" Teddy instigated with a crazy smirk on his face.

"Shut up, Teddy!" I snapped and watched my fiancé laugh into his fist.

"You must wanna die, Peyton. Real shit."

"Nigga, you wanted me to die when you sent them niggas to shoot pass by baby mama's crib. Fuck you!"

"So, what muthafucka?!" Faheem yelled at Teddy then shrugged his shoulders. "Yo' ass still breathing, right?" The room grew silent for a moment then Teddy tackled him to the floor and they started fighting.

Syncere handed me the keys. "P, go start my truck."

"Peyton, you better hide 'cause I'mma fucking kill you!"

Faheem got the best of Teddy and punched him in the face. The gun flew out of his hand. He yelled, "Nigga, get the fuck off me!" Before I could open the front door, Syncere shot at Faheem as he shot at Teddy. I ducked behind the couch.

"Oh, my God!!!" I held my head and covered my mouth. I was praying Syncere was still standing tall. Crawling around to see what happened, my mouth dropped and my eyes grew wide as Faheem's body was slumped to the floor. I instantly went numb.

Syncere ran over to Teddy who was laying against the coffee table while holding his stomach. Helping him on his feet, he told him, "Hold on, cuh. I got you."

"That nigga really got me..." Teddy gargled up blood, fading in and out of consciousness.

"This nigga's just grazed but we still gotta get this nigga to the hospital!"

My feet wouldn't let me move. This shit felt like a fucking movie but it wasn't, this was my fucking life right now. Syncere reached for my hand. "We gotta get the fuck outta here, P."

The two of us got Teddy to Syncere's truck. He was bleeding from his stomach so badly and after everything that just went down, I was scared as fuck. I felt sick. Was Faheem dead? I couldn't stop crying. I couldn't believe he set Teddy up. I was sure there was more to the story but right now my mind was on getting away from all of this shit.

Syncere screeched off, looking towards the back seat at Teddy. "Hold on, cuh!"

"Nigga, this shit burns!"

"You think Heem's dead?"

"Shit, that nigga gotta be. Fuck!" He banged on the steering wheel and drove like a mad man through the streets. Looking between me and the road, he said, "Please stop crying, P."

I held my head and whispered, "I really can't, Syncere. I'm all fucked up. You just..."

"It's all good, P. You gon' be good. I promise you that. We just gotta get this nigga to the hospital and I gotta make a quick phone call."

"It better be Jesus you 'bouta call 'cause..." I watched as he pulled out his phone and scrolled through his contacts. Calling someone up Syncere told the person he needed a favor and to look out for a text in a few minutes.

"Can you slow down?"

"Slow down?" He glanced over at me like I

was crazy. While texting on his phone, he asked, "Do you not see what the fuck just went down? I can't slow down. You got a body in yo' living room, did you forget that shit? I'm tryna take care of that, P. For real, relax, please." Syncere told me, sounding frustrated as fuck.

"Oh, my God. Is this really happening?" I laid my head against the headrest and clutched the seat belt around me. Looking back, I was surprised there was no sirens blaring. I just knew somebody had called the police on us. A bitch was panicking in the front seat. "What the fuck? What the fuck?" I repeated.

"P, calm down."

"Can you just slow down?!"

"We gotta get my fucking cousin to the hospital, man! Can you please calm the fuck down, sweetheart? Please."

"Stop telling me that! I'm trying!" I screamed at Syncere and held my head again. My shit was pounding.

Getting to Doctor's Medical, Syncere dropped Teddy off by the entrance of the emergency room and drove out of the parking lot. We all knew bringing him inside would bring too much heat on the situation. I thought we were going to jail anyway so my ass started praying.

"I hope that nigga be aight, man. For real," Syncere shook his head as he drove along the streets looking zoned out but still holding my hand.

"I can't believe Faheem's...he's..."

"Well, believe that shit. I told you that muthafucka wouldn't be disrespecting you anymore. Plus, he set up my fucking cousin. I had to do what I had to do." He spoke coldly and gripped my thigh. "You know shit's 'bouta get crazy, right? I need you to lay low for a few while I get my game plan together, aight? You done already seen and know way too much as it is and I don't want you getting hurt, Peyton."

"What about my stores? I mean, I can't just up and shut down like that."

"You can and you gon' have to. Just trust me, P." Syncere told me. "I got you."

# SYNCERE

"Good morning or... perhaps not really." The newswoman reported with a heavy British accent and solemn face. "It's just shortly after 6a.m and the residents here of this Carol City neighborhood say they are fed up. Miami PD are investigating and surveilling the area after a man was transported inside Doctor's Medical Hospital drenched in blood. He appeared to be unconscious and just left alone to suffer from a gunshot wound to the stomach. As bizarre as this may sound, that man has since disappeared.

Residents reported they heard chaos and gunshots just after midnight. Police officials state they responded to Doctor's Medical shortly after learning the victim may be in relation to the shooting. However, when the police showed up to the hospital, the medical director told them, and I quote, "the man was treated for his gunshot wound with my best team and moved to recovery." The director later went on to say that his staff, "somehow lost track of the victim." At the moment, the man's name, current condition as well as his whereabouts have not been noted nor released leaving everyone wondering what has happened. This is the neighborhood's sixteenth shooting this month.

Miami PD issued a thorough search of the neighborhood as well as the entire Miami Gardens. They are asking the public for any information on a person stumbling away from the scene. Unfortunately, there were no further details provided at this time. As always WPLG Local 10 will keep the public updated. Reporting live from Carol City this early morning, I'm Jamie Lynn."

I was up watching the news wondering where the fuck Teddy disappeared to and what happened to Faheem's body. I knew that nigga had to be dead when we left his crib so I made a quick call to have him taken care of and P's crib wiped clean. My nigga Bull was supposed to handle the shit now it was looking like I had a war on my fucking hands. Bull was my cellmate for a couple of years until he got out after serving three years for a B&E. Filled with pure Haitian blood, he was tatted up, dreaded up and he always spit that real shit. We got through some tough times behind the wall and I saved that nigga from getting sent to the infirmary a few times while locked up. The respect level would forever be mutual and before he got out, he told me to hit him up if I ever needed anything. With all the fuck shit going down, I figured what better nigga to call in the clutch than an OG like Bull himself.

I didn't need to worry about bitch ass Miami PD sniffing around looking for a dead body and shit. Nah, Bull was supposed to have me covered. Man, I just did eight long fucking years behind the wall. A nigga like me wasn't going back to prison and I was willing to do whatever it took to make sure I stayed a free man. I kept replaying what went down in my head of me pulling up to this nigga Faheem's crib. It's weird as shit how in tune I was with P already because I could sense her get nervous as shit from jump. I just didn't know why but who fucking knew she would tell me some shit like that? That was my dumb ass for not asking for her full name as time went on but shit who knew she was the one this nigga Faheem was dogging out. I'd been working for the man who was hurting her soul and plotting on my blood? This was only gon' get crazier and I felt like the biggest fucking fool for not being more on top of everything to figure it out sooner.

Dropping Teddy off to the hospital had me feeling all types of ways. I should have listened when his ass was going in about being set up. I quickly pushed all that business shit to the side and squeezing that trigger on Faheem's bitch ass meant there was no turning back. The only things on my mind was making sure my cousin pulled through and preparing for what was about to come. I also had to make sure Peyton's mental stayed intact. I knew all of this shit was a lot for her to deal with. That's why I put her ass up in a telly. I needed to keep her away from the craziness for a couple days while I figured some shit out. Low key my head was all fucked up. Shorty really had me gone to the point where I was willing to catch a body for her, like I wasn't already trying to avoid certain troubles.

Looking over at her lightly snoring, I grabbed my phone and walked into the bathroom to make a call. When Bull answered, I asked, "What the fuck happened? I figured you knew how to handle situations like this!"

"Man, when me and my cleanup crew got there, all that was left was blood and shit. There wasn't a body or nothing, Syncere! He explained, hollering back. "Fuck you wanted me to do, play hide and seek all night? Nigga, we cleaned the mess and left."

"Fuck!"

"Next time you call me up with a job, let it be legit."

"I coulda sworn I sent a bitch nigga to heaven, On God!" Pacing the bathroom floor, I contemplated my next moves and decided to keep Bull's ass on standby. "You know what? He ain't the king of Carol City and I damn sure ain't new to this."

"Sounds to me like you done started some shit, Syncere." Bull sighed and asked, "So what's the word?"

"Gimme a couple of days but the next time I call yo' ass, make sure the shit is all the way dealt with."

"Don't worry about my end. I always come through," he told me. "I can keep my ears to the streets for yo' ass."

"Aight good looks." Hanging up, I left the bathroom and noticed Peyton was just waking up. I hoped her ass didn't overhear the conversation. I was plotting to take over Faheem's whole operation. It was time for a real one to step up.

Yawning, she said, "Damn, I guess I dozed off, huh?"

Walking over to her, I sat on the bed and smoothed her wild hair down. "Yeah, you been snoring for like two hours. How you feeling though? You good?"

Resting her head against my shoulder, she replied, "Honestly, I'm still shaken up. I never thought I would actually feel ready to leave Faheem until I met you. You really shot at the nigga for me, Syncere." Peyton lifted her head and gave me a soft smile. "You really fuck with me like that? You really ready to step in and show me love the right way?"

"P, I been tryna do that since the day I met yo' ass."

"Heem ain't dead, is he?" she questioned.

"Syncere, I'm scared this shit is gonna get too crazy and I don't want you to get hurt. Teddy's already fucked up.

"I don't want you stressing none of that, aight? My only concern is making sure you good, P. I can handle myself. Trust me, a nigga ain't want you to see all that."

Looking up at me, she told me, "But I did see it and I'm telling you to be careful. That's all."

Kissing her lips, I said, "I got you." Then, I started laughing a lil' bit. "I can't believe yo' ass really cut a reverend."

"Shut up, that shit ain't funny! I could get locked up, Syncere!"

"You'll be aight, gangsta." I was cracking up when she hit me with a pillow and we started wrestling on the bed. She locked her legs around my waist and I smirked at her. "Well shit, if you wanted some dick all, all you had to do was whip it out, baby."

I watched as Peyton's mouth dropped chest and she licked her lips. I didn't want to make it seem like a nigga was taking advantage of the situation so I let her ass make the first move. She started rubbing all on my dick and I knew it was go time. I was finally gon' hit this pussy. I buried my face between her thighs and sucked on her pussy until she cried and begged for the dick.

"Please, fuck me. I need you like right now."

Slipping on a condom, I felt like the man hearing her say that shit. I felt the same way as I bent her over and started fucking the shit out of her. Slapping her ass, I gave Peyton the meanest backshots. She threw her ass back and grabbed the sheets damn near pulling them off the bed.

"Mmmm yessss, right there..." She moaned all crazy. I cupped her chin and planted a sloppy kiss on her lips then suddenly pulled my dick out. Looking back at me all crazy and out of breath, she asked me, "What you doing?"

Switching positions, I got on top of her then pushed her legs back towards the headboard and held them in place. Fucking the soul out of her, I toyed with her clit and smirked as I watched her body go into convulsions. "Mmmm, a nigga needs this every day and night. Goddamn, P."

"Every day?"

"And every night, baby." I groaned against her ear and gripped her waist. Sweat beads dripped from my foreheat just as I felt her cumming. Peyton moaned crazily with her usually well out together face all screwed up in ecstasy as we came at the same time.

As she attempted to catch her breath, all I heard her say was, "Damn."

"Damn is right. That pussy got some power.

You need to be fucked like that all the time. I don't know what that nigga was doing with all this right here."

Getting up from the bed to toss the condom, I told her, "Come shower with me. I gotta go take care of some other shit. I'll be back in a few to check on you."

P frowned and whined, "You're just leaving me in this telly by myself? I really don't wanna be alone right now, Syncere. With my best friend, Milah, missing in action for whatever reason, you're all I got."

I tossed the condom and doubled back in the room to question what I just thought I heard. "Milah? I know you ain't talking about Teddy's girl Milah?"

"Yeah, how you know her?"

Shaking my head, I told her, "Man, I don't like her ass. Plus, Teddy wants her head 'cause she just got this nigga for a couple hunnid bands and dipped."

"What?! You sure we talking about the same chick? I don't think she would be that dumb." P told me and I described Milah then watched as her mouth opened wide.

"Yeah, I don't know what type of bitches you run with but that one is sneaky as fuck. I'd tell yo' homegirl to be easy out here."

Walking over to where I stood, P looked up at me. "I knew something was up with her ass but robbing Teddy? She ain't even answering my calls either."

"Of course not, she ain't that stupid. But you already know how this shit goes and you ain't getting caught in the crossfire. So like I'm telling you, sit tight and I promise you, I'll be back." I kissed her lips and reassured her, taking her hand in mine.

"Fine, Syncere. I'm trusting you."

"Good. Now, bring yo' ass on in this bathroom girl. And where is this church at that you be going to?"

# CHAPTER ELEVEN

# MILAH

I sat by the windowsill in my uncle's living room getting more paranoid by the minute. I smoked cigarette after cigarette just itching to ditch Quita's ass. Ever since I picked her and her kids up last night, she kept bitching and moaning about being pregnant. My uncle was pissed that we came knocking on his door late as hell at night but desperate times called for drastic measures. Quita's dad popped his shit but he always came through for her. And, it was just my luck that my old nigga, Lucci, slid in my DM on some "let's link up, I miss you" type shit. We fucked around heavy for a few months until he went off to Atlanta to try to start a rap career. I used to tell myself he would come sniffing back around this thang when the shit didn't work out and sure enough, I was right.

As I watched the news waiting for Lucci's ass to hit me back, I thought to myself, *hmm, little do he know, he gon' be my escape from all this shit.* I was sure Teddy was already on to me robbing him and in the moment, I was on some revenge shit so I was carefree. This morning, I was regretting it and knew it was only a matter of time before he called my phone looking for me. His ass probably on the hunt for me. I mean, he wasn't the first nigga I had robbed but he was most definitely the cream of the crop. I still couldn't believe I did that dumb shit but there was no looking backwards no matter how much I was rethinking it.

"Ahh, shit!" Quita doubled over in pain and held her abdomen.

"Girl, if you don't sit down! Shit, you making me nervous as hell." I lashed out at her as I puffed on the Maverick cigarette and roughly ashed it.

"Well, excuse the fuck outta me. I really can't sit still. These Braxton Hicks contractions be serious sometimes." Quita slowly went back to pacing the carpet back and forth rubbing her growing belly. "My daddy's been gone for hours now and he let mad quick after he got that phone call. I hope he's alright."

"I'm sure Unk is fine. Will you just sit the fuck down and relax?"

Rolling her eyes, Quita came to sit down on the couch. She cut her eyes at me and said, "I mean, if we're being technical here, it's your fault I'm this fucking jittery too."

"My fault?"

"Yeah, your fault. You popped up at my mama's house with some money and you been looking over your shoulders ever since." My cousin squinted her eyes at me. "What did you do?"

I was about to answer her when I turned and caught the tail end of a crazy story. "Shhh, hold on. I think they just showed my best friend's street." Turning up the volume on the plasma TV, I joined her on the couch and we listened to the news lady report a shooting and mysterious missing victim that was possible in connection to it. My thoughts went to Peyton to check on her and Faheem but I feared reaching out would somehow get Teddy hip to where I was. It was gon' have to wait. Out of nowhere, Quita started crying.

"Damn, that's my baby's father's hood. I wanna call his ass but he don't give a fuck about this baby and here my ass go crying about him. This shit sucks."

Comforting her emotional ass, I pulled her in for a hug. "Calm down. And who you fuck with that live over there?" At first, I could have cared less but I couldn't front, she had me curious now.

Quita replied, "You know somebody named Marco? That lil' fine muthafucka there..."

"I don't know, Quita. Just try to relax." My phone rang and it was Lucci finally calling me back. Smiling, I answered the call. "Okay then, I see nigga's didn't forget about, Millz."

"Forget you? Never that, baby. You ready for me?"

"I will be in a lil' bit. Gimme like a half."

"Aight, you know a nigga miss yo' fine ass and that pussy."

Quita got up and went to check on her kids just as I laughed my ass off at Lucci's statement. "You shouldn't have left. Ain't nobody checking for you, Lucci, especially not in the damn studio!" I cackled.

Laughing back, he replied, "Yo', you always did have a slick ass mouth. I hope you still know what to do with that pretty muthafucka."

I smirked into my phone. "Yeah, so bring that ass here boy."

"I got you. Text me the address."

Ending the call, I laughed to myself at how thirsty Lucci was and how easy it would be to reel him. Just then, the front door open and slammed shut. My uncle came stomping through the house. I heard him greet Quita in the hallway. "Daddy, I was worried all night about you. Damn!"

"Chiquita, I'm a grown ass man but thank you. I still can't believe yo' ass is pregnant as hell." Turning the corner, I leaned up against the wall and he turned to me. "What's good, niece?"

Nodding my head back at him, I said, "Thanks for coming through, Unk. You always there when it matters."

"That's what family's for. Now, let me get

back to my lady friend upstairs." My uncle headed up the stairs and me and Quita broke out laughing.

"Daddy, you left a bitch up in yo' room this whole time?!"

"Damn Unk, I'm tryna be like you when I grow up," I joked but I was serious. My uncle was a real OG out here. Lucci sent me the looking eyes emoji and I sped this lil' family reunion up. I had a nigga pulling up and new moves to make.

# PEYTON

The minute Syncere left the telly is the same minute everything hit me. I curled up on the bed feeling numb as the tears started flowing. I guess it was reality hitting me in the face. What the fuck was I doing? Did Syncere really shoot at Faheem? Were these muthafuckas about to fight over my ass? Why would Milah rob Teddy? Was it true? My mind was going crazy and I wanted it to stop. I just wanted all of this shit to go away. After years of Faheem cheating on me, it was over. After all the fights with these bitches around Miami, it was over. After all the disrespect, it was over. Every single tear I cried, burden I felt and the sadness that lived in my heart was gon' be a down payment on some new shit. I didn't know what was coming but I knew it was about to be a hell of a ride.

Pulling myself together, I went to shower to let the hot water and steam take me to another place. I needed a fucking vacation but before I got my store back together and my life. It seemed like everything was falling apart to come into place and I was praying it all worked out. As I moisturized and got dressed, my sister popped into my head. She was probably trying to reach me by calling my phone and texting. When I called, she answered on the first ring.

"Hello?"

"Hey."

"Peyton?!" Paris shouted into the phone. "Where the hell are you? I been calling you for hours! Don't make me have to come by your house, baby sister."

"I'm not even home but I'll be aight."

"I didn't ask if you was *aight*. Besides, I may not be as hip as you but your tone is telling me otherwise. Did you get my text the other night? And where are you even at?" She hit me with question after question after question.

Rolling my eyes, I sat on the couch in the hotel room and flicked through the TV channels. "Look, I'm just away clearing my head. I can't believe mama just gon' let the reverend come in and take daddy's place. Paris, I'm all fucked up right now. And then you're pregnant, it's a lot to take in." I told her. "There's so much going on."

"I can't change the fact that I'm pregnant, Peyton! Now, was that your street on the news, P? What's going on?" Paris sighed stressfully. "I swear, you need to leave Faheem's ass alone for good not just for a few hours 'cause he pissed you off. I mean, damn, I know you gotta have more sense than you been showing. He's selfish and dangerous and-."

"Hold up, Paris."

"No, you hold up." She cut me off. "You been losing yourself slowly but fucking surely with all the bullshit going on around you and it always seems like you choose him over your own family. Like, what the fuck is it gon' take for you to put yourself first?"

"I choose him over family? Family?!" Paris was tripping! How dare she come at me with this whole family bullshit? Her ass was at the house the day the fuck shit went down with the reverend. Didn't her ass jump on him? She was acting funny that day and so was my mother! Did she forget she was hiding a whole pregnancy from me after I'd just lost my own baby? At this point, fuck family! Jumping up from the couch, I said, "You wanna stress family to me when you're condoning another man sleeping in daddy's bed. I mean, damn are the sheets even changed?"

"Peyton-"

"Nah, fuck you, *sis*! Look, after today, don't say nothing else to me until you wanna speak some real shit to me. Good luck with your pregnancy." I lashed out and hung up on her ass. I was hot. My sister didn't even know that I had a new nigga and that I was trying to put certain shit behind me. Nah, she was talking out the side of her neck and I had to put her ass back in place. "Fuck this shit..." I grabbed my purse, room key and left.

Although Syncere told me to keep my ass in the telly, a bitch needed some air. Leaving out the Inn, I caught a taxi and told him to just drive.

"Anywhere in particular, miss?"

"No, just drive please." Staring out the window and letting the breeze hit me, I stopped to get some flowers then decided to go past the cemetery to visit my daddy. Placing the flowers on his tombstone, I broke down crying asking him to help me. "Daddy, I need you. Everything is falling apart and don't even get me started on mama." I sobbed, hugging the cold stone. "I wish you were here to make it all better and tell me what to do."

"You need to be strong." I jumped up, once again thinking I was tripping and hearing a dead person talk to me. Turning around, I saw it was my mother. She didn't say anything to me and I didn't say shit to her. We stared at each other for a moment until she spoke again. "Peyton, I'm sorry. I miss him so much." Walking over to her, we hugged and comforted each other. For the first time in months, I felt the love in her embrace and it only made my ass cry harder. "I don't love the reverend. I was lonely and he's a good friend."

"Mama, I can understand that but it hurt like hell to see that go down. And then, the new hair and the clothes..."

Cupping my face, my mother wiped my tears and sniffled. "Pey, I'm sorry. I don't know what I was thinking. I guess it was just grief but I didn't meant to slap you or hurt you. I love you so much, baby. I'll always love my Cal."

"I love you too, mama." I watched as my mother bent down to kiss the tombstone then we walked over to her car. "So what's going on with the reverend? Should I be worried, mama?"

"I've taken care of that, Peyton." Climbing into the car, my mother drove out of the cemetery and I looked over at her. I was scared to ask her for this favor but I had to. If there was one thing I learned in life, there was always two ways to skin a cat.

# SYNCERE

"If it wasn't for yo' ass, I'd probably be dead, cuh."

As soon as I left the telly, I got a call from Teddy asking me to meet him at his crib. Sitting in this his living room looking at him all bandaged up again just made me want to kill Faheem even more. It was like this slime ass muthafucka was fucking with everybody and walking away like he was God or some shit. I needed to put a stop to it all. Puffing on a blunt, I told him, "You know what it is, cuh. But you know we gotta come hard now. Shit just got real."

"You really fucking with P though? Since when?"

Passing him the weed to roll up some more, I replied, "That don't matter and yeah, that's all me. I'mma marry that girl." Teddy laughed at me and held his side as he grimaced in pain. "That's what you get, nigga. How the fuck did you leave the hospital anyway?"

"Man, you know me. When I'm ready to leave from anywhere, I leave. The fuck? I had one of them pretty lil' nurses get all the meds and shit I would need. After them doctors patched me up,

I snuck out the emergency exit and took a cab all the way here."

Shaking my head, I told him, "Teddy, you crazy as hell, cuh. So how you wanna move since this nigga ain't dead yet? We gon' be running shit from now on."

"I feel that. I'm on whatever, you already know that. Plus, I still gotta get this sneaky ass bitch Milah."

"Speaking of, why the fuck you ain't tell me her and P was best friends, nigga? This shit getting crazier by the minute, cuh." My phone rang and it was this nigga Saige hitting me up. "Hold on, this nigga Saige calling me right now."

"Keep it cool."

Answering the call, I said, "What it do?"

"Yo cuh, you heard from this nigga Heem? I been blowing his shit up since I saw the news. Niggas was shooting over that way last night," Saige told me what I already knew.

"Oh word? I ain't been up too long so I ain't even know. But you know yo' brother," I told him. "The nigga probably tied up with a bitch or some shit."

"Damn nigga, all night and morning? Nah, that ain't like his ass. And where the fuck is this nigga Teddy at? Y'all niggas playing and we gotta get to this paper! We was supposed to handle that

Philly shit. I'm calling a meeting, fuck this shit. Be at the warehouse in a few."

Just then, an idea popped in my head and I ran with that shit. I'd hip Teddy to the shit afterwards but for now, I was gon' make it seem like I was still on this business shit. Ignoring my cousin asking me what was up, I told Saige, "Aight nigga, lemme see if I can find this nigga Teddy and we'll be there."

"Aight then, bet."

I ended the call and looked over at Teddy staring back at me. Rubbing my hands together, I said, "Nigga, it's go time. We gon' go up in this meeting like everything is everything but Saige ain't gon' leave that muthafucka breathing." Teddy dapped me up in a brotherly hug and nodded his head. "What you tryna do about this bitch Milah?"

Smirking at me, he said, "Oh, that's already in the works. You tryna take this ride with me in a few?"

"I got you, nigga." Leaving from his crib, we hopped in my Nav and headed to meet this nigga Saige. I didn't know what my cousin nigga had up his sleeve but I had his back regardless. I thought about P and called to check on her but she didn't answer. As soon as I tried calling her again, her ass was hitting me back.

"Where you at?"

"I'm handling some business. Why does it sound like you're not in the room, P?"

She told me, "Listen Syncere, I know 'cause you a thug and all that you think you got all the answers but I may have a better one. I'm trusting you and right now, I really need you to trust me." Gripping my gun, something told me that pretty bitch would be glued to my hand today.

***

Teddy glared at me and turned up the Remy bottle he'd just bought. Grimacing in pain, he held his side and said, "Let's finish this shit." I hit this nigga Saige to tell him we were about to pull up.

"'Bout time. Long time no see Teddy," he said, opening the door and dapping him up. I could tell my cousin wanted to merk the nigga right then and there but he played it cool.

"You still ain't heard from this nigga Heem?" I asked, walking in behind them and heading to the living room.

"Yeah, I did."

As soon as I laid eyes on this bitch ass nigga Faheem sitting in the living room all cool, calm and collected, I raised my gun and so did Teddy. Marco's lil' ass along with one of his homies raised their guns as well.

Faheem smugly asked, "You looking for me, nigga?"

"I knew I shoulda shot yo' ass in the muthafucking face."

"But you didn't!" He hollered. "And if it wasn't for my bitch LaLa, I'd be dead. So what's yo' next move?"

"To kill yo' ass and take over all this shit."

Saige hollered, "Lemme pull the trigger on these niggas, bro!"

Laughing, he asked, "You wanna play with yo' life over a bitch that don't belong to you? You a dumber muthafucka than I thought, Syncere."

"Nigga, I love her ass! You don't and you foul as fuck."

Without another word being said, Teddy's gun went off and Marco's ass dropped. Bullets started flying and this bitch ass nigga Faheem ran out of the living room, shooting backwards. *POW! POW! POW!* I shot at Marco's lil' homie while Teddy laid Saige's ass down. Standing over him, he emptied the clip. "Where this nigga go?" Next thing we heard was sirens, yelling and a bunch of chaos coming from outside.

"Oh shit," I peered through the windows and noticed the police had stopped Faheem in the driveway. They shouted for him to get down on the ground. Grinning, I turned to Teddy and said, "Nigga, we gotta go."

"Go where? Jail? Fuck that, I ain't-"

"Just follow me, we getting the fuck up outta here." Leaving out the basement just in time, we made it back to my truck and I wasted no time hitting up Peyton.

"Nigga, bang this left and-"

"Hold on," I cut him off when she answered the phone. "P, I'm on my way to you but I gotta make a stop real quick, aight?" She told me to hurry up and I put the pedal to the metal.

# MILAH

Leaving out the corner store, I felt like that bitch as I strutted over to Lucci's Altima. I had a purse full of money and a fine ass nigga waiting on me. I opened the passenger door and was met with weed smoke and music blasting. Sliding my ass into the leather seat, I said, "Well, it took you long enough. Good morning."

"My fault, sexy. I had some shit come up but a nigga here now. What's good?" He pulled me in for a kiss and then tried pushing my head down to his lap.

"Damn nigga, can we pull off from in front of the store first? And you promised to take me shopping before we did anything so…" I rolled my neck and cut my eyes at him. If Lucci thought I was just gon' suck his dick right from jump, he was tripping. He sucked his teeth and pulled off.

"You done got feisty as hell, Milah."

"You know how my mouth is, Lucci. Don't be acting surprised. So where you taking me?" Glancing over at him, I noticed he had an attitude so decided to change the mood. "You know I'mma suck that big muthafucka, relax."

Lucci gripped my thigh and said, "Aight. I know a boutique that got some dope shit I think you would look bad as fuck in so we gon' hit that up. Then, I'mma eat you...I mean, feed you."

Laughing, I swatted his shoulder. "Cut the shit. Anyway, I guess could go for some pasta. What you like to eat?"

"Pussy!" I almost choked on my spit when he started laughing.

All that laughing shit faded when we pulled up in front of some cheesy looking storefront. It looked like a Rainbows or some shit from the outside and I definitely wasn't one to shop there no matter what. Not to knock the bitches who did, but Milah just wasn't on that wave. I looked over at Lucci hop out of the car like it was nothing but my ass was stuck when he opened the door for me.

Laughing, he said, "Come on, girl. What you waiting for?"

"This is it?"

"Just come on." He reached for my hand and we headed inside. It looked like a convenience store with the candy and groceries on the shelves. I wanted to run out the store and tell this nigga Lucci to never hit my line again. But my mouth dropped when we stepped in there and I saw all the nice clothes, shoes, purses and jewelry everywhere. "Yeah, that's what I thought. Close ya mouth." Lucci told me.

"I thought..."

"I told you I knew of a spot." He winked and me and hollered out, "Yo Chi-Chi!" A few moments later, a short Asian lady appeared dressed like Mulan but the old bitch was pretty as hell.

"Ayeee, Lucci honey," she greeted him with a warm smile and hug. "How are you? You come back to see what's new, huh?"

"I'm here to drop some bread on my baby right here." He told her while hugging me around the waist. "This is Milah. Milah, this here is my people's, Chi-Chi."

I nodded my head while she said, "Pretty girl, Lucci. Pretty girl," Chi-Chi smirked at the both of us then clapped her hands together twice and said, "Come! I show you all the best. You like dress, hmmm?"

Turning to face Lucci, he blew me a kiss and said, "Come on, baby. Let's get fly together and have a good ass day."

I didn't complain one bit as I grabbed dresses, shoes to try on in the back. Truth be told, her little hidden boutique was the shit and I would definitely be going back. I stood in front of the mirror dancing to some song that played throughout the speakers, feeling myself. "Lucci, baby. You ready to see what this dress looks like? You gon' wanna eat me alive…" I snatched the curtain back to show off the bad ass rose gold dress and was met with a gun in my face.

"You thought you could get away with that shit, huh? Don't you know who you fucking with? I guess not…"

"Teddy," I whispered, feeling my whole body start to tremble. "Please…"

Chi-Chi appeared and he handed her a knot

of money. She looked at me like she just hadn't been smiling all in my face and calling me pretty. Counting the money as she walked off to the front of the store, she said, "Don't make too much mess, Teddy. You know what I mean."

"Lucci, help!!!" I yelled and started crying as Teddy grabbed me by my hair.

Laughing while he pushed me inside the dressing room, he looked at me with an evil smirk on his face. He said, "Didn't be bring yo' ass here? Fuck you calling him for?"

"What?"

"You been thinking with yo' lil pussy instead of that big ass head of yours. Now, where's my fucking money?" Feeling the gun against my temple made me piss myself and Teddy smacked me with the gun, disgusted. "Bitch, keep the same tough ass energy you had when you robbed me!"

"I'm sorry! Please, Teddy. Please!" I begged for my life. My heart was beating like crazy. I couldn't believe Lucci set my ass up and I didn't see the shit coming at all. I thought he really wanted my ass back. I thought I would get away with robbing Teddy. Man, I was wrong as hell and with pee running down my legs and sweat dripping from my forehead, nothing else mattered but saving my life.

"I'mma ask you one last time. Where's my shit, Milah?"

Crying hysterically, I pointed to my purse. "I have most of it but…"

"Most? You think this shit is a game? Man, fuck this shit." Teddy smacked the shit out of me then grabbed his money from my purse. Looking down at me with hatred in his eyes, I knew it was over. All the niggas I had sucked, fucked and came up off, it all came down to this one. *POW!*

# CHAPTER
# TWELVE

THREE WEEKS LATER

# PEYTON

"You sure you wanna do this?"

"Yeah, I'm sure. I'll be back." I kissed Syncere's lips and took a deep ass breath as I climbed out of his whip. Life was crazy but if it was one thing I knew, I finally had a real one by my side and there was no way I was losing out on that. That day when I left the cemetery with my mother, I asked her for the biggest favor I could ever think of. All she had to do was make one phone call to Mr. Arnold and the biggest drug lord in all of Miami was brought down. Fuck starting a drug war, I wanted this shit over with.

Once I convinced Syncere that him and Teddy wouldn't face any jail time, it was nothing to have him go along with the set up. They slapped cuffs on him and pinned all the murders that took place in Saige's house on him. There was no need for a trial and Faheem's ass was locked up facing seventy-five years. See, while his ass reigned over the streets of Miami, the police wanted to snatch him up but could never touch him. I did that. Walking up to the building, I counted my blessings, my family and my new man twice.

"Hi," I greeted the woman behind the tall desk. "I'm here to visit and inmate."

Slapping a pink sheet of paper down before

me, she rudely told me, "Fill out this form. If you need a locker, you'll receive a key. If not, have a seat until you're called. Next!"

"Well damn..." I rolled my eyes and took the notepad. A few minutes later, I was done filling out the basic information the form asked of all visitors and given a number. I impatiently waited to be called, looking around the waiting area. I just shook my head at the pregnant bitches and bitches with babies coming for visits. I was glad to say that wouldn't be my ass. This would be my first and last time coming up here. They called for visiting and we all lined up to go through the metal detectors. Walking into the visiting room, I grew overwhelmed by the amount of females in there and the chatter. I couldn't necessarily hear anyone's conversation but it was just loud as fuck. Spotting someone who looked like Faheem, I walked closer to the booth. We stared at each other until I reached for the phone first.

"Well, don't look so happy to see me," he joked. I wasn't happy though, this wasn't a fucking social visit. I couldn't even speak; he looked so different. His head was now bald and in just a few weeks, he'd lost hella weight. "You came here not to speak?"

Clearing my throat, I said, "I came here to tell you, you lose."

"What?"

"You...lose and I win. For once, I win and I'm gonna be happy."

Glaring at me, Faheem asked, "Be happy with a nigga who stole you from me? Be happy with a nigga who was disloyal?"

"Disloyal? If anybody's ass was disloyal, it was you. All these years, it's been you!" I shouted, trying not to let my emotions get the best of me. My makeup looked too damn good. "I deserve to be happy, Faheem! You just out here making babies on me meanwhile, I lost mine! Have you really sat and thought about how losing a baby could affect a bitch? Have you ever stopped yourself before you decided to do some shit that would hurt me? Have you?! "You put me through a lot, my nigga. The worst! All I ever did was love you. I gave you every part of me and you drained me. Syncere ain't shit like you!"

"Fuck that nigga," Faheem spoke through tight lips, being careful not to draw attention to himself. "I shoulda killed both of y'all muthafuckas for violating me."

Leaning closer to him, I smirked and replied, "Yeah, well, too late. You deserve everything you get." I stood up to leave.

"P!"

"What, Faheem?"

He looked me up and down with pure hatred in is eyes and said, "I never loved you and if it were up to me, you'd be right where yo' fucking daddy is at."

Swallowing hard, I said, "I figured that much but baby, it's a lesson learned. Have fun for the next seventy-five years thinking about the bitch who put you in this muthafucka." Blowing Faheem a kiss, I dropped the phone and walked off feeling unbothered. All I heard was banging against the glass and this nigga screaming for my ass to come back. I was all types of bitches and he was going to get me. Mark his words, he was going to get me. Leaving out of the prison, I wasn't sweating shit. I had God on my side and the law. Plus, a real nigga whose love could be felt just from his touch. Hopping back in Syncere's Nav, I leaned over and kissed his lips.

"Aight, y'all niggas keep that shit to a minimum." Teddy joked from the backseat.

"Shut up." Syncere stepped on the gas and said, "I still don't get why you had to go see this nigga."

"To see his face when I told him what was up." I told him. "Look Syncere, I'm riding off into the sunset with *you* and that's all that matters. The past is the past."

"The past is the past." He nodded his head and drove off. "Now, Teddy, back to what you was telling me about Milah's ass."

Glancing in the backseat at Teddy, I said, "Yeah, I still wanna know how you found my own friend."

Laughing while sparking up a big ass blunt, he said, "Oh, I know how to move out here, cuh. Y'all remember that nigga Lucci from around? He thought he was about to the next Lil' Durk or some shit?"

Syncere rubbed his chin. "Nah, that must've been when a nigga was locked up."

"I remember Milah used to fuck with his ass for a lil' while." I chimed in, curious to know what Lucci had to do with this. "What about him?"

"I kept watching Milah's story on Instagram waiting for her ass to slip up or do something. She shared a pic of them two with the caption "real ones always come back" and even tagged the nigga. So," Teddy puffed on the blunt. "I hit the nigga up and let's just say money talks around this bitch but we already know that shit."

"So what you saying, y'all set her up?" I asked him.

"I'm saying that bitch went against the grain, P! Niggas don't take that shit lightly no matter who you are."

"I don't get how niggas be setting females up like that. I hope she rests in peace, man."

"You know you still like family to me, P."

I sadly shook my head and Syncere held my hand. I mean, yeah Milah was in the wrong for robbing Teddy but I wished the situation could have been handled differently. When I learned of her death a couple of weeks ago, I was in my feelings and couldn't even talk to Teddy's ass. But, at the end of the day, this street shit comes dangerous consequences and we all knew this. He was foul for pulling the trigger but Milah was living foul too. Her death and the fact that she wasn't even given a funeral stunned me but every day it was getting easier.

Syncere pulled over and I made eye contact with him. He said, "I need you mentally here with me right now, Peyton. Fuck everything that ain't in the benefit of us. You see all this shit that went down and we still standing strong? I know it's only been a lil' minute but I love you P. No bullshit, I'd do all of this over again. Hitting the back of yo' car, saving you on the bridge and showing you real love is out there. I fucking love yo' ass."

Holding back tears, I told him. "I know you do. I can see it, I can hear it and I can feel it. That's why I chose you."

"Nah, I chose you."

"Whatever, gimme a kiss." Pulling his face towards mine, we shared a deep, passionate kiss. I forgot all about Teddy's ass in the backseat until he started fake crying. We both looked back at his him.

"That was fucking beautiful," he said, wiping fake tears. "Now, can we hit the fucking airport or nah? The strip club is calling my name!"

It was then I noticed we were definitely heading for the airport. Punching him in the arm playfully, I asked, "Syncere, where are we going and why is Teddy's ass coming too?" I frowned and he broke out laughing.

Puffing on his blunt, Teddy gave us the finger. "Damn, fuck y'all too."

Taking my hand into his, Syncere just

winked at me then said, "I was thinking yo' ass could use a vacation. Shit, me too."

"Now? What about...?"

"Stop worrying and just live in the moment, P." As the sun beamed down, we kissed again at a red light and I wrapped my arms around his neck. Fuck what Teddy's cockblocking ass had to say. If somebody would have told me I'd be riding off into the sunset, literally, with my nigga and his cousin, I would have died laughing. It wasn't exactly a fairytale but it was some real shit.

With no luggage, just the yearning for a break from the craziness, me, Syncere and of course Teddy prepared for takeoff. The captain made an announcement and the baritone in his voice made me listen up and pay attention. He said, "Good afternoon passengers. This is your captain speaking. First and foremost, I'd thank the Lord above for making this trip possible and may be see to it that we take off and land safely.

Welcome onboard Flight 89A, the nonstop flight to Las Vegas, Nevada. The time is approximately 2:45pm. The weather looks good and with the wind beneath the wings, we should expect to land at McCarran International Airport in just under five hours. The flight crew will be coming around in about fifteen minutes or so to offer you a light snack and to select a beverage. This will be an easy going flight with a movie set to begin shortly after takeoff. Whether you're headed out on business or romance, make this trip hard to forget. And that's all, folks. I'll will speak with you all again before we reach our final destination. Until then, just lean back, relax and enjoy the flight."

Looking over at Syncere, I noticed he was mid prayer then looked further down at Teddy who was already knocked out snoring. Butterflies invaded my belly as Syncere slipped his hand into mine. Pinching myself, I couldn't stop smiling. Even though we were on our way to Vegas, I'd already felt like I won. My mother and I were back to normal plus Paris and I were on speaking terms again. I made a mental note to have them look after my stores for a couple of days. On top of everything, I felt like I hit the lotto on love when I opened my heart to a *real* Carol City nigga. Big things were gon' happen and changes were coming. I bowed my head to join Syncere in prayer. *Jesus, please be a fence. Here we go...*

# THE END

# DID YOU ENJOY

'When A Carol City
Thug Loves You'

& You Need More **DOPE** Reads?

# CHECK OUT MY CATALOG!

*Baby, You Can Do Better*

**A BEST SELLING STANDALONE NOVEL**

https://amzn.to/2vjulTr

*Giving My All To A Certified Boss 12*

**THE COMPLETE SERIES**

Part 1: https://amzn.to/2OnQC9r
Part 2: https://amzn.to/2vgJLYI

*His Hood Love Turned Me Out*

**A STANDALONE**

https://amzn.to/3ai4Pxe

Made in the USA
Monee, IL
21 July 2020